Foul Justice

M. A. COMLEY

D1534034

ISBN-13: 978-1505646412

ISBN-10: 1505646413

OTHER BOOKS BY
NEW YORK TIMES BEST SELLING AUTHOR
M. A. COMLEY

Cruel Justice

Impeding Justice

Final Justice

Foul Justice

Guaranteed Justice

Ultimate Justice

Virtual Justice

Hostile Justice

Tortured Justice

Rough Justice (coming Jan 2015)

Blind Justice (A Justice novella)

Evil In Disguise (Based on true events)

Forever Watching You (#1 D I Miranda Carr Thrillers)

Torn Apart (Hero Series #1)

End Result (Hero Series #2)

Sole Intention (Intention Series #1)

Grave Intention (Intention Series #2)

It's A Dog's Life (A Lorne Simpkins short story)

ACKNOWLEDGMENTS

As always love and best wishes to my wonderful Mum for the role she plays in my career. Special thanks to my superb editor Stefanie, and my wonderful cover artist Karri. Thanks also to Joseph my amazing proof reader.

Licence Notes.

Prologue

Trisha Dobbs cowered in the corner. She wrapped her trembling arms around her two small children and kept her gaze on the three men ransacking her immaculate home. "Don't hurt us any more, please!"

The man snarled and ordered, "Get the rope and tie them up."

Trisha gasped, and he turned to look at her, his eyes narrowed. She quickly averted her eyes, not wishing to annoy the man further. She'd already lashed out at him while trying to protect her son and daughter when the three brutes had forced their way into the house. He had a gash above his right eye where her flailing fist had connected, and she had a gash across her cheek where he'd retaliated without hesitation. She'd sensed, then, that she and her children were in for a rough ride and that the man was used to getting his way with women, one way or another.

"Mummy, I want to go toilet," little Rebecca said as tears welled in her bright blue eyes. Trisha comforted the child and kissed her forehead reassuringly.

"Sssh, hon, try and hold on. Go through your alphabet to take your mind off it, like I told you. A is for apple, B is for—"

"Shut the fuck up, bitch," the man snapped, his voice filled with venom.

"I… I'm sorry—" Trisha stopped when the man rushed at her and ripped her daughter from her grasp.

"*Mummy!*"

"No! I'm sorry. Please don't hurt my baby." Trisha sobbed and clung tightly to her two-year-old son, Jacob.

The man picked up Rebecca and roughly dropped her on the large white leather sofa opposite her mother. Trisha soon saw the trickle of yellow liquid drip down the sofa onto the rug below. Sensing danger, she placed a finger to her lips to warn her daughter to keep quiet. Rebecca covered her mouth as her shoulders trembled, and tears cascaded down her flushed cheeks. Too far from her mother's reach, the four-year-old was petrified.

The man in charge towered over Trisha, his body blocking the light from the crystal chandelier overhead. "What time will he be home?"

With the man intimidating her, Trisha found it impossible to think properly. She glanced up at the lion head–shaped gold wall clock hanging above the fireplace. "Dave should be home at any minute," she told him in a quivering voice.

The men had come at eight o'clock, and it was now half past ten. Trisha's husband always arrived home around eleven on match days when he played at home. He generally declined going for a drink with the rest of the team after work. He was the type who preferred to keep out of the limelight, and he hated the notoriety connected with his job. Given the option, he would choose to be home with his family, unlike most of his teammates, who appeared to revel in fighting off the paparazzi at London's elite nightclubs.

One of the men tied her arms behind her back before moving on to little Jacob. Her heart went out to her baby, and wanting to protect him, she pleaded, "Stop! He's only a child. What harm can he do? Please don't tie him up."

Appearing uncertain, the man looked over his shoulder at his boss, who glared and nodded for him to continue.

Jacob cried out in pain as the man roughly wrapped the rope around his fragile wrists.

"It's okay, sweetie. Show Mummy how brave you can be." Trisha tried to reassure him, hoping to prolong the charade that they were all playing a bizarre game.

Soon both children were sobbing uncontrollably, and Trisha, numb with helplessness, felt as though she'd been stabbed numerous times in the chest. *My God, what can I do to get out of this?*

"Go upstairs and start on the bedroom. Tear it to pieces if you have to," the man in charge ordered.

Trisha tried hard not to give anything away with her facial expressions under the man's intensive stare. She felt confident the gang wouldn't find the safe tucked under the floorboards in the master bedroom, but considering the mess they'd made of her beautiful home since their arrival, anything was possible.

The man in charge took a step toward her. "If you don't tell me where the jewellery is, I'm gonna start hurting the kids."

Knowing she couldn't delay the inevitable any longer, she sighed. "In the back bedroom."

"Where?"

"In the wardrobe. On the shelf, there's a box."

He leaned close and ran his thumb from one side of his throat to the other. "If you're tricking me…" Jacob was sitting beside her, and the man yanked the boy's head back. "He gets it, you hear me?"

"Yes, I understand. My jewellery is in that room. I don't have much. You think we're rich, but we're not. This house is mortgaged to the hilt. All our furniture is on hire purchase. Dave doesn't make the kind of wages reported in the papers, I swear," she told him between sobs. *Stay strong for the kids' sakes.*

"You think I've got 'fucking idiot' tattooed on my forehead, bitch? What do you take me for?"

"I'm sorry. It's the truth. You *have* to believe me."

"Oh, do I now? You blondes are all the same—thick as shit! You think you can wrap us men around your fingers, don't ya?"

Trisha remained silent.

The man went into the hallway and shouted up the stairs, "The spare room at the back, in the wardrobe, on the shelf. Let me know when you find something."

Trisha squeezed her eyes shut and tried to visualise what jewellery she had put in the specific box. Her heart sank when she remembered she'd placed nothing spectacular there. All her best jewellery, Christmas and birthday presents that Dave had bought her, were safely tucked away under the floorboards. She hoped and prayed the children wouldn't give her away, for all their sakes.

"Something wrong?" The man was in her face again, his eyes glinting with pure evil.

She wanted to be her usual sarcastic self, but the present time wasn't appropriate. "No. Just hoping Dave returns home soon."

"So am I," he said, before releasing a full belly laugh.

A few minutes later, the other two men returned to the living room and handed the box to the man in charge. He slammed down the glass of brandy he'd poured himself on the nearby side-table and marched towards her. "Is this *it*?"

She gulped. "Yes, I told you, we're not wealthy. I—"

"That's bullshit, lady, and we both fuckin' know it. Where is it? This is your final chance or the kid gets it."

Words stuck in her throat as the three intruders eyed her with contempt. Suddenly, the man in charge reached out and yanked Jacob to his feet. The man pulled out a knife and placed it against her terrified son's neck. Trisha watched in horror as the blade sank into her child's skin, and droplets of blood trailed down onto his white T-shirt, followed by his terrified tears.

"Please! I'll tell you. Don't hurt my baby."

"I'm waiting."

"In the main bedroom—you have to move the bed—there's a small safe in the floorboards under the rug."

He nodded for his men to go back upstairs and check. Seconds later, he received a shout that they'd located it, and seconds after that, little Jacob lay in a heap on the shag carpet, his throat slit from ear to ear.

Chapter One

"Come on, lazy bones. Time to get up." Tony tapped Lorne on her bare behind as he walked past and disappeared into the bathroom.

"Why? Why did I agree to start today? And why did you get me drunk last night? I've got the mother of all hangovers, now."

Tony laughed and started singing his latest annoying song in the shower.

Lorne, happy at last, smiled and sat up in bed. In a few weeks, she and Tony were going to get married. *Just a few more things to organise.* Her life was on the up for a change, after all she had encountered over the last few years.

Tony came back into the bedroom and caught her smiling. "You should do that more often, it suits you."

"You cheeky sod, I'm always happy." She picked up his pillow and threw it at him.

He caught it, aimed it, and hit her full in the face. Tony cocked an eyebrow at her. "You are?"

"When I'm with you, yes." Lorne smiled and fluttered her eyelashes.

"You're such a creep, Detective Inspector."

She puffed out her chest, proud and pleased that she had decided to return to the Metropolitan Police, despite losing her wonderful partner Pete almost two years ago. However, the job came with a proviso, one that she wasn't relishing. She was expected to break in a new partner, to train him to think on his feet and ensure he carried out the job in the manner to which she was accustomed. All under the watchful eye of Sean Roberts, her detective chief inspector. Butterflies took flight in the pit of her stomach as she reminded herself what lay ahead of her that day.

"Hey, what's up?" Tony asked, his frown matching hers.

"Nothing. Just thinking."

He approached the bed and sat beside her. Picking up her hand, he placed it to his lips and tenderly kissed it. "About Pete?"

That was what she loved about Tony, his intuitiveness. He knew exactly what she was thinking—most of the time, anyway. He was one of the most sensitive men she'd ever met, and she regarded him, after several failed relationships, as her soul mate.

She cleared her throat and stroked his cheek with her free hand. "You're so perceptive."

Tony shrugged. "I should be. It goes with the job. Now get a wiggle on; you don't want to be late your first day back."

Lorne took a leisurely shower, her mind full of anxious thoughts, the most prominent of which was her father's warning that, 'Going back doesn't always work.' Only time would tell on that one, but in the meantime, she'd do everything in her power to prove him wrong.

After leaving the Met, she hadn't stepped foot back in the station where she'd worked the previous eight years. She had settled into a new life of renovating houses. After she finished refitting the kitchens and bathrooms and doing a general tidy-up, she would be looking for good tenants who wouldn't trash the properties, but she was prepared to sell to recoup costs if she couldn't find suitable tenants.

Approximately two weeks before, Lorne had been having a lazy Monday morning, going through the necessary paperwork that accompanied her new career, when the persistent ringing of the doorbell had interrupted her.

"All right, all right. Keep your knickers on."

Her mouth had dropped open when she saw Detective Chief Inspector Sean Roberts standing on the doorstep, looking kind of sheepish.

"Sir—I mean, Sean. What the hell are you doing here?" He hadn't contacted her since she'd resigned and left the force, so her surprise was genuine.

He gave her an embarrassed smile and looked over his shoulder at the road behind him. "Umm… Getting wet at the moment. Any chance I can come in for a chat?"

"Of course. Sorry."

Her former boss followed her through to the kitchen where Henry, her eight-year-old border collie, rushed up to greet him.

"In your bed, boy," Lorne told her four-legged companion. Wagging his tail, he trotted back to his squidgy bed, sulked and moaned when he threw himself down. "Typical man. He likes to have the last word."

"He remembered me." Sean smiled nervously.

Something didn't fit right. Sean appeared uncomfortable, awkward to be there. Lorne had never seen him like that, not even during their relationship years before.

"A coffee would be nice?" he asked hopefully as she sized him up.

"Gosh, where are my manners? I'm so shocked to see you." She filled the kettle and motioned for Sean to sit at the kitchen table. "Milk and sugar?"

"You mean you can't remember?"

She blushed at his teasing. "Why are you here, Sean?" She picked up the milk carton and poured a few drops in both mugs.

He responded as she eased into the chair opposite him. "I want you to reconsider and come back to the Met."

"You're kidding me?" She almost dropped her mug on the table.

"Nope. It took a lot for me to come here and ask you, Lorne, especially after the way you handed in your resignation."

Dumbfounded, she said, "My views haven't altered."

"I can understand that. Just like I understood where you were coming from when you handed your letter to me. It was tough, losing Pete like that."

She dropped her gaze to the table, determined not to show him how affected she still was by her partner's death. *You can't work with someone for almost eight years and watch them die in your arms and dismiss the residual pain and guilt with a mere click of your fingers.*

Clearing her throat, she looked him in the eye. "I don't understand why you're asking me to return, then."

"To be honest, I'm a man down... Yes, I know, you're a woman, but you know what I mean."

With her interest piqued, she leaned across the table and asked, "So what happened to DI Paul Marsden then?"

"Umm... He wasn't up to the job, and that's all I'm prepared to say about him. So?"

"What about Superintendent Greenfall?"

"Let's just say he realised what a good copper you were when it was too late."

She laughed at the irony behind his words. He studied her while she got her laughter under control. "I'm not sure, Sean. I have a whole new career now. And... er, Tony and I are due to get married in a few weeks."

He seemed stunned by the news, if only for a second. He recovered quickly. "Wow, congrats. You don't waste much time, do you?"

It was her turn to be shocked. "What do you mean by that?"

Looking shamefaced, Sean chewed his bottom lip for a second or two. "Nothing." He quickly turned the conversation back to the reason for his visit. "So how about it? The thing is, I need a quick answer; otherwise, I'll have to advertise internally."

Silence filled the kitchen for a while, and Lorne thoughtfully sipped at her mug of coffee. She took in the worry lines she'd never noticed before around her ex-boss' grey eyes.

"Lorne?"

"Good God, Sean, you can't turn up here after having no contact with me for almost two years and expect me to answer a life-changing question within a few minutes. I have Tony to consider, nowadays. All our decisions are made jointly."

Reluctantly, Sean stood up and looked down at her. "Fair enough. Can you give me an answer by the end of my shift tomorrow?"

"Still working nine-to-five, are you?" She laughed, trying to break through the chill that had materialised between them. He'd never been the type to do less than a sixty-hour week.

"Hah! That'd be nice. Maybe if you came back to work for me, it would ease my workload a little." He held up his hands. "Not that I'm putting any pressure on you, of course."

They walked up the Minton-tiled hallway to the front door. "Of course not. I promise to get back to you tomorrow, Sean, either way. Thanks for asking. Oh, and it was good to see you again after all this time," she added, hoping to make him feel guilty for avoiding her over the past few years.

She and Tony had spoken at length, weighing up the pros and cons of going back to work with Sean and her old team. Her fiancé's final words on the matter were, "Give it a go. If things don't work out, you can always leave and pick up where you left off with the renovations."

So, there she was, her first day back in paid employment with the Met. After quickly bolting down a piece of buttered toast, Lorne left the house and set off to her new-old job.

Chapter Two

Lorne parked her Nova in the station car park at five minutes to nine and stood, glancing up at the station for a few minutes, trepidation tingling along the hairs on her neck.

Come on, girl. As Ty Pennington would say, 'Let's do it!'

Not much had changed in the drab reception area. A few of the uniformed coppers nodded their heads in acknowledgement and recognition. Walking up to the desk, she was saddened to see Sergeant Harry Watson standing erect behind it.

"Everything all right, ma'am?" he asked, looking perplexed.

"What? Oh sorry, Harry. I was expecting Sergeant Harris."

"Ahh… Bert retired at the end of last year, ma'am. Can I just say it's good to have you back?"

Lorne smiled and nodded. "Of course he did. I'll have to drop by and see him when I get five minutes—and thanks, Harry. That's kind of you." She shrugged and pulled a face. "I'll tell you at the end of the week if it's good to be back."

The sergeant buzzed her through the secure door, and she walked up the concrete stairs, through the grey dingy hallway to the incident room. When she opened the door, Sean stopped addressing the group of officers in the Serious Crime Squad, and everyone turned to look at her. A moment's silence filled the room before AJ started clapping. Before long, the room had erupted into applause, and Lorne battled to control the flush turning her cheeks beet red.

Sean approached her, took her by the elbow, and guided her into the room. They came to a standstill in front of the whiteboard that she assumed the DCI had been writing fresh notes upon. Sean raised his hand, and the room fell silent again.

He cleared his throat and announced, "Lorne, on behalf of the gang, welcome back. You've been missed."

Glancing around the room, she saw her old team nod their heads in approval at the DCI's words. But one person, a young woman at the back, was giving her a hard, cold stare.

"Thanks, Detective Chief Inspector Roberts. It's good to be back, I think. I've missed all you guys, too. Now, let's get to work, shall we?" She'd never been one for idle chitchat during working hours, and her team knew that. She just hoped they remembered it and hadn't let their standards slip in her absence.

Sean took over. "I guess the first thing I should do is introduce you to a new member of the team. Katy, step forward please." The woman joined them, apparently grudgingly. Lorne stretched out her hand to greet Katy as Sean introduced them. "Sergeant Katy Foster, this is Superwoman herself—otherwise known as Detective Inspector Lorne Simpkins, your new partner."

The pair shook hands. Lorne smiled, while the other woman's mouth remained set in a straight line. Lorne made a mental note to find out the officer's background from Roberts after the meeting was over.

Roberts seemed to ignore the sergeant's strange behaviour. "Okay, Lorne. Do you want to take a seat over here? I'll fill everyone in on a new case that cropped up overnight. Feel free to butt in any time to ask questions."

Both women sat down as Roberts ran through the case.

"At some time just after eleven last night, Dave Dobbs returned to his house in Chelsea to find his two small children murdered and his wife fighting for her life."

Chelsea? Lorne asked, "That's a pretty well-to-do area, sir. Are we talking a wealthy family, here?"

Sean smiled, obviously pleased to see her police brain kicking into gear within minutes of being back on duty. "Yes, Inspector. When I tell you that Dave Dobbs is a premiership footballer, you'll get an idea of the kind of money we're talking about. Here's where it gets interesting: the proprietor can't understand how an intruder could get into the house. The place has state-of-the-art security. Okay, there are no dogs on guard, because they had young kids, but they have CCTV, and no one could get in the gates without knowing the code," Roberts said, pointing to the notes he'd written on the board.

"Are there any nearby neighbours? Did they see or hear anything?" Lorne asked.

"Not sure, as yet. I want you to go out there first thing, Inspector, to walk the scene. I'm not sure what the neighbourhood is like, whether it's close-knit or not—I suspect the latter, since Dobbs had all that security. None of the neighbours have been questioned yet. I'd like you to organise your team to go house to house. It's all we've got to go on at the moment. SOCO are at the house now; Joe Wallis is in charge over there. He's relatively new, so you won't know him. Any other questions? Bear in mind, this is all we have to go on at this time."

"How bad is the wife? What's her condition? And what happened to the kids, sir?" Lorne asked quietly.

"The wife, Trisha, is on a ventilator. She was stabbed repeatedly. I'm waiting on a doctor's report as to how bad she really is. And the kids—Rebecca, aged four, and Jacob, aged two—had their throats cut."

"Jesus, have you had any other incidents like this in recent months?" Lorne asked, her professionalism uppermost despite her eyes misting up with tears at the thought of the pain and suffering the little mites must have been subjected to. In all her time in the force, she'd never come across such a crime. She'd encountered heinous crimes of murder and rape—her own teenage daughter had been a victim of the latter—but she'd never actually come across a burglary where the criminal had killed two innocent toddlers.

Sean Roberts shook his head. "Not that I know of. I've instructed Molly to check the database to see if anything else flags up in another area."

Lorne looked around to find Molly in the room and gave her a quick smile. Molly, a brunette in her mid-thirties with whom Lorne had had severe problems in the past, smiled back and gave a thumbs-up.

"Right, any other questions?" Roberts asked, scanning the room.

The room remained silent.

"Very well then. Lorne, I'd like to see you in your office for five minutes, and then you can instruct your team on what you want them to do next." Roberts was already walking in the direction of Lorne's office.

Her stomach clenched as she stood on the threshold of the room she'd once shared with her dead partner, Pete. Roberts watched, expression concerned. Lorne sucked in a deep breath and could've sworn she smelt Pete's Cool Water aftershave lingering in the doorway with her. Was it possible he was there to lend a helping hand?

"Everything all right, Lorne?"

She took a hesitant step into the room. "Yeah, just a few memories I have to contend with."

Roberts grimaced. "If I could sort you out another office, I would, but these renovations seemed to have ground to a halt with all the cutbacks going on at the moment."

She laughed. "Hey, maybe my builders could lend a hand."

"That's right. I forgot you're into that sort of thing now. What's happening with that side of things? Is Tony taking over the reins?"

"No. We're seeing how things progress here first—"

"Whoa! You mean you don't think this is going to work out?" Roberts said, shocked.

"I don't have a crystal ball, sir. There's no telling what might happen. My builders will continue to work on the properties under the guidance of the foreman. I bunged him an extra £50 a week. I can catch up with things on the weekend, provided I'm not expected to do overtime. And before you make promises you can't keep, I know that whether I get time off or not depends on how a case is going. I'm not that green."

"It's good to have you back, Lorne. I've missed your feistiness and 'tell it how it is' attitude. Your predecessor was so far up his own backside... Well, you know what I mean. I think he had a sense of humour bypass in his dim and not-so-distant past."

She laughed. Feeling less tense, she walked around the desk and sat in her old chair. Yes, she was back. *Now what?*

She remembered Katy's cool greeting. "This new sergeant, what's her background?"

He sat in the chair opposite her and steepled his fingers, as he usually did when he was contemplating something.

"She was transferred from the Manchester force, just passed her sergeant's exam. This will be the first case in her new role."

"So, as well as returning to work after a two-year absence, it's up to me to babysit a new recruit, too?"

Sean chuckled. "She's hardly young, Lorne."

"Are you kidding me? She's barely out of nappies. She must be what, twenty-three?"

"Very good. She's twenty-two."

Lorne whistled and shook her head. "I've never known a sergeant that young, sir. What's the story?"

The DCI winced and said quietly, "She's a friend of Superintendent Greenfall. Well, she's not, but her father is. She's got a bit of a chip on her shoulder. I thought you could knock her into shape in your own inimitable way."

Stunned, she stared at him open-mouthed before she recovered. "Christ, welcome back to the lion's den, Lorne, and don't forget to suck up to your new *novice* partner. She's your nemesis' protégée. If you don't tippy-toe around her, you know what will happen."

She could tell Roberts was struggling not to laugh.

"Sums it up nicely, I'd say," he said jovially, as he departed the room.

Why did she have the feeling she'd been duped?

Chapter Three

Lorne issued her team its tasks and set off for the crime scene with new recruit Katy Foster alongside her.

At the reception desk, DCI Roberts had left the keys to a Vauxhall Vectra that was parked alongside her small Nova in the car park. It was late September. The trees were beginning to turn rich golden and bronze. The autumn rain and high winds were bringing hundreds of leaves to the ground, making the roads and pavements hazardous.

As they headed out to Chelsea, Katy hadn't said a word after fifteen minutes in the car. Lorne decided to speak first. "So, Katy, how long have you been down here? DCI Roberts told me you were based in Manchester."

Staring at the road ahead of her, Katy replied, "A month."

Her tone held an edge that didn't sit well with Lorne, but she continued the conversation nevertheless. "You're very young to be a sergeant. You must have impressed your superiors."

"Yep," came the younger woman's abrupt retort.

Lorne navigated the heaving London traffic before trying again. "Do you have a boyfriend?"

"Yep."

Lorne bit the inside of her lip, forcing back the anger she feared would escape the next time she opened her mouth. Although she herself was known for her feistiness, she'd never been rude with it. Katy was striking her as rude. Glancing out the corner of her eye, she saw that Katy held her back rigid and her arms folded tightly across her chest. *One final attempt, and then if she doesn't answer, well...*

"So has your boyfriend stayed up in Manchester, or has he come down here with you?" Lorne made certain that the question required more than a one-word answer.

"Yep, he's back there."

Ah ha! So that might be her problem; maybe she was missing him.

"Is he going to join you down here?"

"Maybe."

Anger bubbled near the surface, but they arrived at the Dobbses' house. Annoyed, Lorne ordered tersely, "When we get inside, I want you to stay by my side, okay?"

She heard Katy expel her breath and *tut* noisily. Lorne wanted to grab her by the shoulders and give her a good shake. She hated insubordination. She'd always run a tight ship with a supporting crew—except for Molly, but Lorne had even turned *her* around, come the end. The trouble was that she'd have to tread carefully where Katy was concerned, due to the Greenfall factor.

This situation sucks!

Pulling up to the gates a uniformed officer approached the car. She showed him her warrant card and introduced Katy.

"Very well, ma'am. If you pull over to the left there, it'll ensure the SOCO team can leave the scene without obstruction once they're finished."

"I'll do that. Thanks."

The house was huge. Lorne guessed that the large red-bricked mansion house dated back to the Victorian era. The front garden was mostly laid to lawn and bordered with mature shrubs that ranged in colour from golden yellow to deep plum. Her father, once an avid gardener, would be in awe of this beautifully tended garden.

The two women stepped out of the vehicle. Lorne opened the boot to look for plastic shoes for them to use. She could've kicked herself for not coming prepared; her old car would've been kitted out properly. Yet another job to add to her to-do list.

"Damn it. Nothing," she told Katy, who only shrugged in response, making Lorne's annoyance and anger intensify.

When they approached the front door, one of the Scene of Crime officers was at his vehicle. Lorne asked him for some plastic shoes, which he retrieved from the back of his van and handed to her.

"I'm looking for Joe Wallis. Is he still here?" Lorne asked the officer, a man in his early–mid thirties, as she slipped on the blue plastic shoes.

"In the bedroom upstairs, ma'am. We're almost finished here," the officer told her.

"Dare I ask if you've found much?"

"I'd rather you ask Wallis that, ma'am," he replied, giving her an awkward smile.

"I understand. Thanks for the shoes. Come on, Sergeant."

Stepping through the front door, Lorne looked up at the magnificent vaulted hallway and galleried landing, decorated in a stark white that had splashes of red in the form of vases, picture frames, and curtains. The modern look was totally different to what she'd been expecting from the exterior of the property.

With her warrant card in hand and Katy behind her, she made her way up the grand sweeping staircase towards the master bedroom at the end of the hallway, passing by several open doors *en route*. Lorne glanced in the rooms as she passed and marvelled at how beautifully decorated they all were, even the two children's bedrooms. One room was bubble gum pink and had a canopied princess bed along one wall, while the other had a mural of a castle painted on the wall. The bed had chains on either end, as though it were a drawbridge that lowered and rose when required by its keeper, who sadly was no longer with them.

Several of the SOCO team, dressed in white paper suits, were still hard at work in the main bedroom when they entered.

"Joe Wallis?" Lorne asked the suited man nearest the door.

"Over here. And you are?" The goatee-bearded man was in his mid-forties, his hair on the cusp of turning grey. His brown eyes glistened in the artificially lit room.

Lorne proffered her hand, but he held his gloved hands uppermost and shrugged.

"I'm Detective Inspector Lorne Simpkins, SIO of the case. Can you tell me what you've found?"

"Sure, I'm almost done here. Give me a couple of minutes, and I'll walk you through the house."

"Thanks." Lorne stepped back into the hallway and stood against the wall. Katy stayed in the doorway, watching the SOCO officers carry out their work.

"Have you worked on a murder case before, Sergeant?"

"Once or twice."

Lorne eyed the younger woman, trying to figure her out. Katy was fairly pretty, didn't wear much makeup, and had olive skin with what Lorne thought were acne scars. She was slim, about the same size as Lorne in height and build, but Lorne noticed that her mahogany brown hair had the look of being pampered and cut by an expert hairdresser.

"You want to be more specific about your experience?"

Katy shrugged and kept her eyes trained on the room in front of her, another thing Lorne hated and considered rude. Finally, Katy replied, "We have murders up there, too, you know."

"Did I say you didn't? Look, Katy. If we're going to wor—" Lorne stopped when Wallis came marching out of the room and down the hallway.

"Come along, Inspector. I haven't got all day," he called over his shoulder as he disappeared downstairs.

"Never mind. Come on." Lorne trotted after Wallis.

The two women walked through the double glass doors into the lounge. Wallis stood by the French doors that led out onto the terrace and pool area. At his feet, the cream carpet had a bloodstain the size of a large beach ball.

"This is where the boy child died, Jacob Dobbs. His hands were tied behind his back, as were his mother's."

Wallis walked to another area and indicated another blood spot on the carpet half the size of the last one. "Trisha Dobbs was stabbed here, at least ten times—how she survived, I'll never know, but she did. And over there—" Wallis pointed to the white couch approximately ten feet away. "That is where the little girl, Rebecca Dobbs, was found. Like her brother, the poor mite's throat had been cut."

"Don't you think that's odd? That both children were killed like that, and yet the mother only had stab wounds. I say *only*, but you know what I mean."

"I agree, most odd. Maybe the intruder wanted to make the mother suffer before and after," Wallis said frankly, as if he'd already thought deeply about the circumstances and possible motives of the criminals.

Lorne looked at all three spots again, her mind racing with probabilities. "You mean, you think the mother was *intentionally* left alive?"

Wallis' mouth turned down, and he nodded. "That's how it looks to me. Otherwise, why didn't she suffer the same fate as her children?"

Lorne's brow furrowed. "Do you think the intruder knew the family? Was it some kind of punishment, perhaps?"

"Now that, Inspector, is something you need to find out. The place was torn apart, both in here and upstairs in the bedrooms. I'd say they were after jewellery, but it's possible they could've been after something else. The best person in a position to answer that would be Mr. Dobbs."

"Have you found any fingerprints?" Lorne asked.

"Yes, but we won't know if they're the family's until we run the tests. There's also a glass. Looks like brandy in it; maybe the intruder poured a drink while he was here. Again, we'll run the usual tests on the glass and get the results back to you ASAP. That's as much as I can tell you, Inspector."

"Who's the pathologist on the case, do you know?"

"Patti Fletcher. She took over from that French guy... Jacques Arnaud, dreadful situation." Wallis' expression was pained.

Unfortunately, Lorne knew all too well whom he was talking about and the case he was referring to. Baldwin, otherwise known as The Unicorn, had blighted her life for almost nine years before she had resigned from the force. Not only had he killed her partner, Pete, and abducted and raped her daughter, Charlie—he'd also put an end to the relationship she had considered leaving her then-husband for.

"Inspector, are you all right? You've gone very pale." Wallis pulled her out of her reverie.

"I'm sorry. Jacques Arnaud was a dear friend of mine. As for the bastard who— let's just say I got my revenge, and he got what was coming to him."

Wallis chuckled and slammed the heel of his gloved hand against his forehead. "Of course. I should've recognised your name. It's an honour to meet someone as famous as yourself, Inspector."

"Ha! I hardly think fame comes into it, Joe. At the end of the day, I was just doing what I was paid to do. Let me correct that— actually I wasn't on the payroll then, but it was still a pleasure to track the bastard down. Can you let me have the results as soon as you get them back?"

"Of course, Inspector. Right away. I'll be on my way now, glad to know that London is safe in your hands once again."

"I doubt that's true, Joe. There will always be some lunatic out there trying to outsmart the police." She looked around her and swept her arm over the scene. "See what I mean?"

"You're right about that. Speak soon, Inspector." Wallis turned and marched out the front door.

Lorne spotted Katy's expression. "What's the puzzled look for?"

"What did he mean?" Katy asked quietly.

"About what exactly?"

"About you being famous. Are you some kind of celebrity?"

Lorne couldn't help laughing, but her face straightened when the images of Baldwin's contorted, vile face shot through her mind. Then she jumped on the chance to pull the moody sergeant into line.

"Let's just say when people double-cross me, they live to regret it."

Chapter Four

Lorne and Katy returned to their vehicle an hour or so later, after they had walked the crime scene, which hadn't told them much apart from where and how the victims had died or—in the mother's case—been beaten.

"What are we going to do now?" Katy asked as Lorne eased the car out of the Dobbses' long drive and through the gates.

"You tell me."

Katy sharply turned to face her. "What?"

"Come on. If you were lead investigator on the case, where and what would you do next?" Lorne asked, her eyes locked on the road ahead of her.

Katy shifted uncomfortably in her seat for a few seconds, then sat bolt upright. Out of the corner of her eye, Lorne saw the younger woman extract something from her jacket pocket: a black notebook.

"Well, I think our next stop should be the mortuary."

It was the longest sentence Katy had strung together since they'd met, and although going to the mortuary was the wrong course of action, Lorne was pleased that Katy seemed at least to be taking her role seriously and thinking about the case, despite her moodiness.

"Why?"

"Excuse me?" Katy retorted.

"You heard, Sergeant. Why?"

After another couple of minutes shuffling in her seat, Katy mumbled, "Because I thought it would make sense to get the post results first."

Lorne could tell Katy was downhearted, so at the earliest opportunity she pulled the Vectra into the nearest lay-by. She pivoted in her seat to face Katy. "It really wasn't a trick question, Sergeant. If we're going to be partners, I'll be expecting you to contribute to the partnership. Yes, I'm your superior; but as the saying goes, two heads are better than one.

"There'll be times during a case where your knowledge will be greater than mine. Don't forget I've been out of the force for nearly two years. Things change, procedures change. I'll be expecting you to voice your opinions, however daft they may seem. In my experience, it's normally the daftest ideas that prove to be the most important part of solving the case. Okay?"

"Yes, ma'am." Katy's voice was subdued, and her eyes never left the road in front of her.

That lack of reaction frustrated Lorne. "Another thing: I don't do moods. Yes, I might throw the odd hissy fit now and again, but I don't put up with moods from my colleagues. Got that?"

Katy shot her a look that said 'I don't give a damn what you say; I've got Superintendent Greenfall behind me.'

And in that instant, Lorne knew she would have more than a few problems ahead of her until she managed to turn the new recruit's way of thinking around.

"I said, '*Have you got that*?'"

"Yes, ma'am. Message received."

"Right. Oh, and while we're having this little discussion, I'd also like to say that my door is always open. I don't expect any member of my team to go through problems alone, but I draw a line at personal problems affecting the workplace and the equilibrium of the team. You got a problem inside or outside of work, I want to hear about it first, not second-hand, okay?"

"Yes, ma'am," came Katy's usual toneless response.

Seething inside, Lorne started the car again and kept her voice buoyant. "Next stop *is* the hospital, but *not* the mortuary. If ever there are live victims found at the scene, they need to be interviewed first and foremost. Then we continue on to the post-mortem.

"You were almost right, though. Six months under my wing, and you'll be set for another promotion." Lorne laughed, trying to cut through the chilly air circulating the interior of the car, but the stubborn sergeant was having none of her attempts to be friendly.

The rest of the journey to Bart's Hospital remained silent, at least on Katy's end. Lorne however, turned on the CD player and started humming and tapping her fingers on the steering wheel to an old Motown CD someone had left in the machine. She was determined not to get sucked into the sergeant's moody silence.

* * *

The car park at the hospital was heaving, and spaces were virtually non-existent. After driving around the perimeter a few times, Lorne collared a security man, flashed her warrant card, and asked him where she could leave the car. He pointed to a spot in view of his little hut and promised to keep an eye on the car while they went inside.

Their heels clip-clopped along the corridor of the hospital as they made their way to the Intensive Care Unit. Lorne shuddered when she thought of how much time she'd spent either visiting or recovering in hospital over the past few years. It wasn't her favourite place to be, given the choice.

The blonde petite nurse behind reception welcomed them with a broad smile and pointed out the room where Mr. and Mrs. Dobbs could be found.

"Can you tell me how Mrs. Dobbs is doing?"

Her smile vanished and was replaced by sadness. "She's stable for the moment. I'm afraid it could go either way, Inspector."

"Let's hope she pulls through."

Lorne eased the door open to a private room off to the left. The room smelt like a beautiful summer garden when the two detectives walked into it. At least twenty bouquets of flowers of all shapes and sizes were dotted around the room.

Mr. Dobbs looked up when they entered. He sat in an easy chair next to the bed, his wife's hand clutched between both of his.

Lorne introduced herself quietly and showed her warrant card. "Sorry for your loss… Do you mind answering some questions, Mr. Dobbs?"

The man was in his late twenties, with a slim build and a pretty boy face. His eyes were bloodshot and had red rings around them from where he'd been crying.

"Not sure I can tell you much, Inspector. Who would kill my babies like that? Or do this to my wife? We've never harmed anyone. Why?"

Lorne clasped her hands in front of her. "That's what I intend to find out, Mr. Dobbs. What time did you get home last night?"

"Just after eleven. After the match, I always go straight home."

"When you arrived home, did you see anyone at or near your house?"

"No. I knew something was wrong as soon as I saw the gates open."

"And they were definitely shut when you left the house?"

Dobbs nodded and bent to kiss his wife's hand.

"What time was that?"

"I left home about five thirty."

"Where were you playing this evening?" Lorne asked, her throat clogging up. The man obviously loved his wife. He could barely take his eyes off the battered and bruised body lying in the bed in front of him.

"At Greenbank. We were playing Chelsea in a reserve game."

"Was your wife conscious when you got home?"

"No. I called the ambulance straight away. Her breathing was ragged. I rang the ambulance, and they told me what to do to keep her alive."

"I see. So you saved her life. That's commendable. Tell me: Are you contracted to a security firm?"

"What do you mean?" Dobbs asked, puzzled.

"Sorry, I meant the house. I noticed you have security cameras, et cetera. Do you have a contract with a firm?"

"Yes. God, my mind's all over the place—I can't think what they're called."

"Never mind. Is there someone else we can call to find out that information? Would your club know, or your manager, perhaps?"

"Yes, my manager, Stuart Russell. He'll know. Here…"

He handed Lorne his mobile, and she scrolled through his contact list until she found Russell's number. "Jot this number down, will you, Sergeant?" Lorne read the number aloud.

Katy wrote the number in her notebook and then cleared her throat. Lorne glanced at her, sensing she wanted to ask a question. Lorne nodded for her to go ahead.

"Mr. Dobbs, who knows about your security other than your manager?"

The man stared long and hard at Katy and frowned. "I'm not sure what you mean."

Katy hesitated, and Lorne jumped in to clarify what her partner had asked. "Is it common knowledge at the club what security measures you have in place?"

"Oh, I see. I don't make a habit of discussing my personal life with the other players. I don't suppose it would be too difficult to work out what type of security I had, though."

"One final question, and then we can begin our investigation. It's a sensitive question, but a necessary one all the same. Last night, did you identify your children?"

"Sorry, I don't understand. You don't think they were my children at the house?" Dobbs asked, confusion written across his face.

"Sorry, I'm trying to make sure you don't suffer any more than necessary, Mr. Dobbs. When the police arrived at your house, did you make a positive ID of your children? If not, then I'll have to ask you to accompany us to the mortuary at some point in the near future to do it."

Tears spilled from the man's eyes, and he nodded slowly. "Yes, unfortunately they were my little angels that were slaughtered in my home."

Lorne reached out and touched his forearm gently. "I'm sorry. Please forgive me; I had to ask. We'll leave you in peace now. Here's my card. As soon as your wife wakes up, can you call me? The sooner we track down the culprit or culprits the better. It won't bring your children back, but it'll go some way towards healing your wounds."

She knew that to be the case from experience.

Chapter Five

Next stop was the mortuary, and Lorne really wasn't looking forward to that. During the lift ride down to the basement, her insides had started churning to the point of her wanting to throw up. *Get a grip, girl. Hold it together.* Once or twice, she caught her new partner eyeing her suspiciously. She shrugged and explained, "I don't feel comfortable in tight spaces."

Lorne headed for the pathologist's office. She knew it well from her relationship with Jacques Arnaud.

The office was empty, so Lorne headed up the narrow corridor to the suite where the post-mortems were carried out. Looking through the porthole, she saw a woman pathologist leaning over a child's body on the examination table. Lorne tapped the door quietly and held up her warrant card at the window. The woman looked up, waved a bloody hand at her, then indicated that they should get changed into their protective clothing and join her.

"You all right with this?" Lorne asked Katy as they slipped into their -surgeon green trousers and top.

Katy looked a little unnerved, from what Lorne could tell. The reddish usual tint to her cheeks had diminished.

"To be honest, I'm not sure," Katy replied, stiffly.

Oh, great. Not another wimp like Pete! Before his demise, Pete always remained near the door. He had his own designated chair ready to catch his fall when his knees buckled beneath him after the smell of death reached him.

"If you'd rather not go in, I'd understand. I wouldn't like it, but I can't make you go in there."

They'd taken off their heels and put on the flat disposable shoes provided before Katy spoke again. "It'll be my first post. I can't really say how I'll react in there, but I'm willing to give it a go."

"That's all I can ask. Any problems, give me the nod, okay?"

"Yes, ma'am."

"Come on, then," Lorne said, leading the way.

They both walked into the suite and approached the table in the centre of the room. Lorne introduced them to the pathologist and gave a brief nod of acknowledgement to Bones, the assistant who used to work alongside Jacques.

Lorne noticed that Katy looked anywhere but at the cadaver.

"Good to meet you, Inspector. I've heard a lot about you," Patti Fletcher spoke with a smile in her voice—something hard to do, given the circumstances.

"Is this one of the Dobbs children, umm… Miss Fletcher?"

"It's Mrs. Fletcher, but I insist on being called Patti at work. No airs or graces on my watch. And yes, this is Rebecca Dobbs, poor child."

"Terrible case. What do you have so far?" Lorne's gaze drifted down to the child's body, which had been opened and exposed under the pathologist's knife.

"She had her throat cut like her brother. I also found some contusions on both upper arms. She was roughly treated by the perpetrator. It's inconceivable any human being would treat an innocent child so badly."

"Was she sexually assaulted?"

The woman shook her head and let out a sigh. "Thankfully not."

Lorne felt relieved. "What about the boy, Jacob? Have you carried out the exam on him yet?"

She had a good feeling about the new pathologist. Lorne liked her easy manner. She wasn't stuffy like so many of her other colleagues; even Jacques had needed taming when Lorne first met him. It had taken several months before she was able to hold any kind of proper conversation with the Frenchman. After that, things had developed into a deep friendship, before…

Patti's voice drew her back to the present. "Yes, he had his throat slit, but I didn't find any other marks on his body."

"That's a relief."

"Indeed. I hear their mother was fortunate to escape with her life, although rumour has it that it remains touch and go, whether she'll make it or not. It must have been torturous for her, seeing her children manhandled and their lives ended in such a cruel way."

"I agree. The thought of it doesn't bear thinking about. Let's hope she was unconscious before she witnessed their murders. I'll wait to hear from you with regard to the reports then. Any idea how long?"

Patti glanced up from the child's body. "Should have the report ready by the end of the day, Inspector. Like I say, it should be an open-and-shut case on the two children."

"Very well. Nice to meet you, Patti. I'd say I'll look forward to working with you in the future, but… well, you know what I mean."

"Indeed. I'm sure our paths will cross soon enough. Be in touch later."

Lorne and Katy stripped off their greens in the locker room and left the building. On the drive back to the station, Lorne asked, "How do you feel?"

"Actually, better than I expected. Couldn't handle posts all day, though. Even the feel of the post-mortem suite made me shudder."

"Yeah, it's not the warmest place on the planet, granted. You did well."

Lorne glanced out the corner of her eye and saw Katy smile and puff out her chest. *Maybe things aren't going to be so bad between us after all.*

Chapter Six

"I managed to drop the gear off this morning."

He eyed the younger member of the gang, Carl, thoughtfully. "Did Stan say he could shift it?"

Carl shrugged and threw himself into the easy chair in the corner of the room. "No problem. He said he'd ring you when he'd found a safe home for it."

The other two gang members laughed and high-fived each other, but he glared at them and shook his head. "This ain't a game, you tossers!"

He stormed out of the messy lounge and headed up the hallway to the kitchen. He hated the shithole, but it was a convenient place to meet up after a job. He preferred to be tucked up in his own swanky surroundings out in the sticks.

He'd be back there soon enough. One more job that night, and they'd need to back off for a bit anyway. Too many 'convenient' jobs taking place, and the cops would start making some connections. Nope, he'd make sure that didn't happen on his watch.

Taking a can of lager from the fridge that was stacked with four-packs instead of food, he headed to look out the back door, checking the jungle of a garden attached to the tiny two-bed terraced house that belonged to Carl.

He contemplated what lay ahead of them that evening, running through the plans he'd spent the morning going over with the other members. Everyone had been issued their specific jobs. The other two men were still upset at how the previous evening had turned out, but what the heck. *To get anywhere in life, you have to take chances—if that includes people getting hurt, then so be it.*

He jumped when Zac snuck up behind him and asked, "What's up, big man?"

"Nothing. Why, should there be?" he replied stiffly.

Zac was the type who needed a leader: useless and incapable of doing anything apart from taking a piss by himself. Twenty-eight going on sixteen, he'd always been slow at school, a pupil stuck in a class full of dunces and kids unwilling to knuckle down at lessons. But Zac was his brother, and blood was thicker than water. At the moment, Zac had his uses. He knew how to handle a car if they got caught up in a high-speed chase with the filth.

"Just asking, bro. You look distant. Is it 'cause you killed the nippers?" Zac grabbed a can of lager from the fridge.

Killing the kids had affected him more than he was willing to let on. He'd never killed before, but something in him had snapped. The woman shouldn't have pushed him like that. He didn't appreciate folks treating him like a fool. Zac was the fool, not him.

In the end, she got her comeuppance and some. She'd envisage that knife slitting her kids open for the rest of her days. *Serves her right.*

"Nah, they deserved it. So did she. Sorry you didn't get a piece of her."

"Yeah, so am I, she had a nice arse!"

Both men laughed before sipping from their cans.

He grew serious again. "You okay with tonight's job? Anything you're not sure about?"

Zac screwed up his nose and vigorously shook his mop of red hair. "Nah, I'll be right. If I ain't sure of anything, I'll ask. You know that."

"Get set to go at seven p.m. then, right?"

Zac mock-saluted his brother and downed the rest of his lager.

* * *

The afternoon had proved to be fruitless for Lorne and her team. The house-to-house enquiries produced zero information. All the neighbours either lived behind high walls or at the end of long drives, so their sense of community was practically non-existent. The only good piece of news they'd uncovered was that Molly had found out the name of the security firm.

As usual in those types of cases, clues were thin on the ground, and Lorne knew only too well that it would take a few days for anything positive to surface that they could sink their teeth into. She drove home and stopped at the local off-licence to pick up a few bottles of wine.

After seeing the post of Jacob Dobbs, all she wanted to do was snuggle up on the couch with Tony for the evening—after she'd rung her daughter Charlie, that is.

"Hi, Tony. I'm home," she called out as soon as she opened the front door. She was greeted by the scent of garlic, a strange smell she couldn't distinguish, and the sound of clattering pans coming from the kitchen. A smile touched her lips as she bent down and slipped out of her shoes. Wriggling her toes, she massaged some life back into her tired feet. Her first day back had been tough both mentally and physically.

Tony wasn't known for his exploits in the kitchen. He'd been a bachelor for years before they had met. Being an MI6 agent, he mostly ate in restaurants or on the run, or tucked into a tin of cold beans for his dinner. Lorne had been teaching him how to cook over the past couple of months, and that night was his first attempt at going it alone. He'd asked for her opinion on what he could cook, and she'd suggested a spaghetti bolognaise as the safest bet to avoid any food poisoning.

"Help!" Tony shouted from the kitchen, amid more banging of pan lids.

Stifling a grin, she called out, "I'm coming, sweetheart."

"Hurry! Everything is going to pot, so to speak."

Lorne casually walked into the kitchen and headed straight for the back door. She flung it open for Henry to escape the steamed-up kitchen. He scooted past her and stood on the patio, looking up at her, with his tail tucked under his belly.

"What are you trying to do, wreck my kitchen?"

"Sod your kitchen! Help me save the pasta—spaghetti— whatever it's called."

She wanted desperately to laugh at the state he'd worked himself into. Thick beads of sweat had formed on his forehead and were cascading down his face and dripping off the end of his nose into the bolognaise sauce.

Yuck! I have to eat that? Not on your nelly, mate. A full-scale sabotage was needed.

Trying to keep a straight face, she asked, "Did you boil the spaghetti in water? I didn't think you needed to be told to read the packet for directions. Anyway, I showed you what to do."

He gnawed at his lip and widened his eyes in alarm. "Shit! I knew there was something missing."

"Look at the state of my pan. I'll never get that off. This will have to be thrown out now."

"Babe, I'm sorry. What can I say?"

Tony held out his arms, and she walked into them, smiling as she placed her head against his chest. "You can offer to buy a take-away."

"God, that's a given. It's the least I can do, princess."

She knew she should've been angry and ranted at him, but he looked so vulnerable and sexy she couldn't find it in her heart to chastise him. What was the cost of a few pans in the grand scheme of things? "Hey, at least you tried. Most men don't."

Tony pushed her away from him and searched her eyes. "You're a wonderful woman, soon-to-be Mrs. Warner." He slowly lowered his head to hers, their lips met, and the bolognaise sauce started coughing and spluttering behind them. "Damn!"

"Go and sort the take-away out and I'll get rid of this lot." She turned the stove off, withdrew the pan with burnt offerings in it and emptied the contents in the bin, then watched her fiancé leave the room, his shoulders slumped in defeat.

She said a sad farewell to her expensive copper-bottom pots, and they followed Tony's attempt at dinner into the bin, before she rang her daughter.

"Hi, sweetie. How was school?"

Charlie sighed heavily. "Mum! You ask me that every day. Can you change the record, *please*?"

Lorne cringed, knowing her daughter was right. "I'm sorry, but how was it?"

"You're impossible. I can see why Dad left you now. He's right. You do take your work home with you." Despite trying to sound annoyed, Charlie chuckled.

"You cheeky mare. You wait till I see you. All right with your dad if you stay here the weekend?"

"You bet. Whatchya got planned?"

Since she only saw her daughter at the weekends nowadays, Lorne liked to spoil her and take her out to a restaurant on Saturday evenings. The rest of the time, Charlie usually sorted out their fraught itinerary. Lorne and Charlie were hardly ever home either Saturday or Sunday. It was going to be tough being a full-time copper and a part-time parent on her days off. She knew that in the future, there wouldn't be much time for her to 'chillax' as Charlie would say, on the weekend with a good film or book.

Lorne smiled at her daughter's eagerness. "Well, I haven't checked with Tony yet, but what about going ice skating?"

"Wow, yeah! Where?"

"One of the builders mentioned the other day that he takes his kids to the Alexandra Palace Ice Rink. We could have a meal in town afterwards, maybe?"

"Can't wait, Mum. You're the best. I'm gonna hang up now and pack my bag for the weekend."

Laughing, she reminded Charlie that it was only Tuesday, but the teenager had already hung up. Lorne was still shaking her head when a forlorn-looking Tony reappeared in the doorway.

"What's up?" he asked.

"Nothing. Just had a conversation with a very excited teenager, that's all."

He tilted his head and rested it against the doorframe. "Excited about what?"

"Ah, I said we'd take her ice skating on Saturday." Lorne frowned when his gaze drifted to the back door. Something was up. "Tony?"

"Can we discuss it later, like after dinner?"

She walked over and stood in front of him. Their eyes met. "Now you're starting to worry me, Tony."

He pulled her into his arms and kissed her hard. She could feel him shaking slightly and knew how out of character that was—he *was* a tough MI6 agent, after all. Backing away, she placed her hands either side of his face and waited for him to speak.

Tony expelled a heavy breath. "Sorry, princess. I have to go away."

She swallowed and tucked her hair behind her ear, nervous. "Okay... Where?"

"Afghanistan." He squeezed his eyes shut, as if expecting her to explode.

Lorne dropped into a nearby kitchen chair, surmising she hadn't heard the worst part yet. "Why?"

Tony knelt on the floor and looked up at her. "Simon was killed in action whilst on a mission, and I have to take over."

Chapter Seven

Several minutes of silence echoed round the kitchen. Lorne swallowed. "Why you? Can't somebody else go?"

Tony rubbed her cold hands in his and then traced a finger down her colourless cheek. "There isn't anybody else."

She forced back the tears threatening to fall, leaned forward in her chair, and placed her forehead against his. "What about the wedding? How long is the assignment for? Oh, Tony, why you?" Fear gripped her heart and squeezed it tightly.

"It should be a quick in-and-out job, sweetheart." He tilted his head and brushed her lips with his.

"When do you leave?"

"Tomorrow. The plane with Simon's body arrives at Brize Norton at about three. It's going to be a quick turnaround." His voice was filled with sadness that was reflected in his face.

Lorne knew he didn't want to leave her. For the past several months since they had tracked down Baldwin, Tony had pleaded with Headquarters to let him stay in the country on local assignments, instead of the usual overseas cases, until an opening in MI5 came up. Up till that point, they had fulfilled his request and only last week had told him that a transfer to 5 was imminent. *Now this!*

Lorne's shoulders slumped. "Babe, what about the wedding?" She tried not to whine the words but failed miserably as they somehow got stuck in her throat.

"That's two weeks away. HQ have this bastard nailed down in Kandahar. Hopefully I'll make the kill and come straight home."

"You've got to *kill* him?"

"Lorne, you know how these things work." He smiled reassuringly.

"Yeah, I guess. But the Taliban… won't they be more vigilant? On the lookout for other MI6 agents now that Simon's been killed? He must've got close to them."

She was liking the sound of Tony's dangerous trip less and less, and his response of a shrug did nothing to quell her fears.

He kissed her again and hugged her tight. "Hey, I've been at this game for more years than I can remember now, and no one has managed to do away with me yet."

She sighed in resignation. "Okay... We'll have something to eat, and then I'll help you pack a bag." He tutted, and she scowled. "What, I can't even do that for you now?"

Laughing, he stood up. "If it'll make you happy. Although it doesn't take much to shove a few T-shirts and sweaters into a bag."

Just then, the bell rang. "You get the door, and I'll get the plates and cutlery," she told him.

"Deal."

She stood for several seconds, watching his back as he marched up the hallway to open the front door. She'd grown to love that man so much in the past year. It hurt to be away from him. *Is that what true love really means?* How she was going to cope when he left for Afghanistan, she had no idea. She had genuinely never known that love could rule someone's life as much as it did hers and Tony's. They'd spent endless hours discussing the depth and value their lives meant to each other.

Walking back into the kitchen, while Tony answered the door for the delivery guy, she shuddered and picked up the plates and cutlery. *He'll be fine. He'll be back before you know it. Now don't go getting all maudlin. It's his last night. Let's make it special.*

They ate their chicken korma and rice in the lounge in front of the TV. Tony absentmindedly turned on the BBC news. A reporter was out in Afghanistan, telling the viewers that a couple of British soldiers had been killed in an IED incident. They looked at each other, fear filling their eyes. Tony grabbed her hand and kissed it.

"What have I told you? I'll be fine. While I'm away, you're forbidden from watching the news, you hear me?"

She felt the bubbling emotions threaten to show themselves. She stood up. "I hear you. I'll put Henry out, and then I'm going to bed."

"Mmm... sounds like fun," she heard Tony say as she left the room. She found Henry jiggling around, waiting for her at the back door.

The night was fresh and clear, and the stars glistened as far as she could see. Picking out the brightest star, she whispered, "I'm depending on you to look after him, Pete. Bring him home to me, safe and well." Feeling blessed that she had someone on the other side to help guide Tony on his mission, she whistled Henry in and closed the door behind them.

That night their lovemaking was filled with tenderness and fraught desire, after which they spent the night entwined in each other's arms, almost afraid to let go of each other.

In the morning, Lorne considered throwing a sickie at work so that she could travel the seventy-odd miles to Oxfordshire to drop Tony off at the RAF base. But he'd persuaded her not to and instead had waved her off on the doorstep. She'd held back the tears, not wishing him to take that memory of her away with him, but as soon as she had driven round the first corner, she pulled over and wept. Luckily she wasn't the type to wear heavy makeup, so when she arrived at the station and looked in the ladies' room mirror, the damage was minimal. Slight red rings surrounded her hazel eyes. She took a tissue from her handbag and held it under the tap to create a cold compress, then placed it over her eyes for a few seconds.

When she looked at her reflection again, her eyes had returned to near normal.

Lorne left the toilet and walked into the incident room to see people frantically scurrying past. "AJ, what's going on?"

The young man looked up at her and grimaced. "We've had another burglary overnight, ma'am."

"I see. Any victims?"

"Yes, ma'am. One nipper deceased, and his mother stabbed multiple times and left for dead."

"Jesus!" *I guess I'm going to be too busy around here to feel sorry for myself while Tony's away, anyway.*

Chapter Eight

The phone on her desk was ringing off the hook when she walked into her office. She answered DCI Roberts, "Yes, sir. Just got in myself. Can't tell you any more details at the moment. Would you like to sit in on the meeting?"

He sighed down the phone. "Fill me in after, Lorne, will you?"

By the time she finished her call, the team had gathered ready for the team meeting.

"AJ, do you want to fill us in?" Lorne asked.

The young six-foot male left his seat and took up a position alongside the whiteboard, his black marker pen in hand, and started jotting down notes. "Yes, ma'am. At approximately eight thirty yesterday evening, the home of premiership footballer Les Kelly was broken into. When he returned home after a Cup match, he found his son murdered and his wife beaten, stabbed, and left for dead. Again, early signs are that there is no evidence to be found at the scene. The house was turned over; valuable pieces of jewellery and art were reported missing by Mr. Kelly."

"Sounds like the same MO. I take it the security was in place? As with the Dobbses' house?" Lorne asked the detective sergeant.

"Yep, same firm and everything. The house is in a different area, but same kind of setup with regard to the neighbours. Again, the large gates were open when Mr. Kelly got home."

"What condition is the wife in?"

"I rang the hospital as soon as I heard, ma'am. They told me she keeps drifting in and out of consciousness."

"Thanks, AJ. Did you check on Mrs. Dobbs' condition, too?"

"Yes, ma'am. No change there. Mr. Dobbs spends every hour of the day with her."

Lorne nodded. It was good to hear. All the footballers she'd read about in the Sunday papers had bad reputations, partying till all sorts of hours and fooling around on their wives or girlfriends. She'd even heard of a case recently where a player had set fire to his home—his *rented* home—after letting off fireworks in the bathroom. Most footballers came across as having far too much money, while desperately lacking in the common-sense department.

"Okay, let's get this investigation going. I want background checks on both families and the security firm. Something sounds off with that firm. Two incidents within forty-eight hours, and their security was defective *both* times? Yes, get me the info on the security firm, and I'll drop by and see them myself after lunch. DS Foster and I will go over to the Kelly's house first thing. Anything else?"

"No, ma'am," AJ said, already walking back to his desk.

After dishing out the tasks to her team, Lorne stepped into her office and rang Roberts to update him on the new incident.

"I take it you're heading over to the crime scene?" Roberts asked.

"Yep. I'm on my way over there now, sir."

"Keep me posted, and Lorne?"

"Sir?"

He paused. "How's the new recruit working out?"

She laughed. "Depends. You mean me or Katy?"

"Seriously, how's the sergeant doing?"

"She started off a little distant yesterday, but come the end of the day I think I made some headway with her. Why was she promoted and then moved? Can you tell me that?" Lorne asked, absentmindedly tidying her desk.

"You're on your way over to the Kelly's house now. Be sure to let me know when the path reports are in. Talk later."

Lorne was left glaring at the phone. *Hmm... avoidance tactics.* Roberts' avoidance of her question left her wondering what DS Katy Foster had been up to.

Chapter Nine

Lorne tried not to think about her conversation with DCI Roberts on the journey over to the Kellys' house. She was the type of person who made her own mind up about her colleagues, anyway. His words had put a seed of doubt in her mind, though, which meant she'd be watching the DS carefully from then on.

They arrived at the Kellys' mansion just after nine thirty a.m. The forensics team was still in full flow: marking out, measuring, and taking photos of the crime scene. Joe Wallis approached them as they entered the house in their plastic shoes.

Lorne nodded a brief hello. "A member of my team says we're looking at a similar scenario on this one, Joe."

He nodded and his mouth pulled down at the sides. "Everything points to the same MO at first glance. Of course, we'll still have to run the tests to check."

"Can you walk us through the scene?" Lorne looked around the lounge. The furnishings made it a virtual replica to the Dobbses' house. *Does that mean they had the same designer?* She took out her notebook and noted it down.

"Of course. Shall we start upstairs?" Joe asked, snapping his gloves at the wrists. They walked slowly into a beautifully decorated child's bedroom. On the walls was a forest scene, and the bed had been rustically made out of tree trunks. The green-coloured quilt cover, made from what appeared to be a waterproof fabric, had a pool of deep red blood in its centre.

"The child, Lewis, was found dead here. We haven't come across any shoe or finger prints as yet. These are smart cookies we're dealing with, Inspector."

Lorne looked at the scene thoughtfully for a moment, then nodded. "They'll slip up sooner or later. They usually do."

"No doubt. The mother was found in the master bedroom."

Wallis led the way out of the bedroom and up the landing. A couple of his colleagues were still *in situ*, taking photos and dusting for any likely prints. One of the crew looked up and shook his head. Lorne took that to be another negative for possible DNA clues. The case was beginning to get to her, which frustrated her.

"Mrs. Kelly was found in a state of undress, lying face down on the bed. The fact that she was stabbed numerous times in the back rather than the front probably saved her life."

They had to be thankful for small mercies, then. "Any idea what size blade we're looking at?" Lorne asked as she surveyed the room, which again looked as if both families had employed the same designer. *Themed rooms for the kids, and sumptuous décor in browns and golds for both master bedrooms.* She even spotted a couple of vases that looked similar to the one found in the Dobbses' bedroom. She made another note in her notebook.

"Short blade, I'd say, by the amount of blood found. Of course, I haven't seen the victim yet," Wallis said.

With her pen poised ready to note down the answer, Lorne asked, "Have you met the husband? Was he here when you arrived?"

"No, he went to the hospital with his wife. He was in a dreadful state, apparently."

"Okay, we'll take a trip to the hospital. I need to check on Mrs. Dobbs, anyway. Thanks, Joe. Let's hope we don't bump into each other again too soon." Lorne smiled.

When the two detectives returned to their car, Katy seemed puzzled.

Lorne started the car. "What's up?"

Katy squinted at Lorne. "I saw you making notes back there."

"And?"

"I'm hazarding a guess they were about the designer?"

"If that's your guess, then I suppose I'll have to tell you that you're right. What did you pick up?" Lorne asked as she pulled the car to a halt at the traffic lights.

Katy fidgeted in her seat, cleared her throat, and said, "I think we should look into the security aspect deeper. I also think whoever the designer was on both properties needs to be investigated, too."

Impressed, Lorne looked sideways at her and smiled. "Exactly what I was thinking. We'll check in with Mr. Kelly at the hospital, see what he can tell us, and then go visit the firm that carried out the designs and the one who was supposed to be looking after these guys with their 'state-of-the-art' security."

Katy's face didn't even crack into a smile to reflect hers; instead her focus reverted to the traffic ahead of them.

The autumn wind was pretty fierce by the time they arrived at the hospital. Lorne took the comb out of her bag and tidied her hair before they walked into the private room belonging to Mrs. Kelly.

The woman lying in the bed was sporting two black eyes, and her nose appeared to be broken. A bandage was wrapped around her head, and tubes were attached to her nose and her arms. Sitting alongside her was a blond man in his late twenties. His bare arms displayed the latest trend for footballers, a sleeve of brightly coloured imaginative tattoos. He looked distraught, and his hair stuck up as though he'd been constantly running his hands through it.

"Mr. Kelly?" Lorne showed the puzzled man her warrant card and introduced them both.

Remaining seated, he looked at his wife and ran a gentle hand over her brow, pushing back a few strands of blonde hair that had escaped the bandage. "She's never hurt anyone. Why her? Why our son? What has a three-year-old boy ever done wrong?" His voice trembled.

Lorne walked forward while Katy stayed near the bottom of the bed. "I'm sorry for your loss, Mr. Kelly. I'm afraid I don't have the answers yet as to the whys and wherefores for this invasion of your home. Do you mind if I ask you some questions?"

He nodded. "Can't say what I'll be able to answer, though."

Lorne proceeded, her voice calm. "Would you care to run through what happened when you got home last night?"

"We had a match. I play for Borthwick City—not sure if you're aware of that." Lorne nodded, and he continued in his broad London accent, speaking quietly as if to avoid waking his poor wife. "I got home between eleven thirty and eleven forty-five. We were playing the Arsenal at their gaff. The gate was open when I got home. It's *never* open. Sandra gets scared when she's on her own. Usually a friend comes to sit with her, but Kim had something else on last night... Oh God, I should've rung her to tell her. She'll be devastated."

"That's okay. Give me the number, and we'll contact her when we get back to the station. Please, go on."

He took out his mobile and looked up the number of his wife's friend, then placed his mobile in Katy's outstretched hand. She noted down the number and handed the phone back to him before he continued. "I rang Sandra at halftime—"

"Sorry, what time was that?"

He clenched his eyes shut as he thought. "About eight thirty, I suppose."

"Did you speak to her?"

"Yes, she'd just tucked Lewis… She'd put him to bed and was watching TV in bed." A stray tear coursed down his cheek and he wiped it away in anger. "Why—why would they do that to him?"

"I promise you I'll find out. One last question—well two, actually. How long have you lived at the house? And can you tell me who your designer was?"

Again he paused to think. His gaze rose up to the white-panelled ceiling of the private room. "We've been there just over two years. I don't know who the designer was, sorry; that's Sandra's department. She dealt… I mean *deals* with that kind of thing."

Lorne gave him a reassuring smile. "Not to worry. We have other leads we can follow up on."

Tilting his head slightly, he asked, "What do you mean? You think the designer is involved in this somehow? Other leads… Oh my God, the club said something had happened at one of our reserve boys' houses. Is this to do with it?" His face drained of all colour.

"I can't say for certain if there's a connection, Mr. Kelly, but it's an angle we'll be investigating. You say the club didn't tell you to take extra precautions or anything?" Lorne found that piece of news astounding, and she intended to delve deeper into why they had deemed it *unnecessary* to warn the other footballers at the club. She made a mental note to ring the director of the club.

"No, nothing. They said that there had been a slight incident and Trisha Dobbs was in hospital, end of! What the fuck are they playing at? If they knew—my boy died because…" The young man buried his head in his hands and broke down.

Lorne stepped forward and rubbed his shoulder gently. "Leave it with us, Mr. Kelly. Again, I'm sorry for your loss. Here's a card. The minute your wife comes round, will you ring me, please?"

He swallowed and gave a short nod. Lorne and Katy left the room. "Shit, what callous bastards are we after here? That's two families they've ripped apart, and for what? Some jewellery!"

"We don't know if anything was taken from the Dobbses' house or not," Katy reminded her.

"You're right. We need to catch these bastards before they destroy another family. That much is clear. While we're here, we might as well call in to see if Mrs. Dobbs has regained consciousness yet."

They took the stairs up one flight and stopped at the top. As far as they could see, there was some kind of commotion going on outside Mrs. Dobbs' room. Mr. Dobbs was standing outside, looking around him in bewilderment. Lorne and Katy ran towards him.

"What's happened?" Lorne asked breathlessly.

A faint look of recognition crossed his face. "It's Trisha."

Lorne shook his arm and pleaded, "Mr. Dobbs, what's going on?"

"She's come round," he said. The words travelled from his mouth along with an expelled breath.

"But that's wonderful news, isn't it?" Lorne asked, perplexed.

His head swivelled as he watched another doctor and a couple of nurses sweep past them and enter his wife's room. "But, she doesn't... she can't... remember me. She has no idea our kids are dead. Oh, my God. How the hell am I going to tell her that?"

Chapter Ten

Downhearted by this strange and unwanted turn of events, Lorne drove back to the station deep in thought.

As they got out of the car and headed through the front door, Lorne asked, "I'm about to start issuing the team with tasks. What angle would you like to concentrate on?"

"Really? You're willing to let me loose on something?" Katy sounded amazed.

"Start saying things like that, and I'll get reservations about it. So?"

Katy stalled at the bottom of the stairs. "Do you mind if I tackle the security firm?"

Lorne was pleased her new partner had chosen the option she had wanted her to take. She had a feeling the security firm would balk and fight their corner, and how Katy reacted to that would show Lorne a lot about what type of character she was, and how much balls the girl had.

They walked into the incident room, and the place was buzzing with activity.

"Everything all right? Anyone got any progress they want to share?" Lorne asked, scanning the team. A couple of them raised their hands, as if they were back in school, while they continued talking on the phone.

Katy went to her desk while Lorne approached AJ; he was just hanging up. "I've got the details of the security firm for you, ma'am. I haven't made contact with them, as you said you'd do that. A couple of the guys are going over the backgrounds of the footballers involved, and nothing is really showing up as yet."

"Give the details to Katy, will you, AJ?"

"Ma'am?" the young detective asked, giving her a puzzled look.

"The security firm details, DS Foster is going to be dealing with them. Is that all right, AJ?"

AJ's cheeks reddened, and he glanced away, appearing embarrassed that he'd challenged her. "Yes, ma'am."

Lorne patted him on the shoulder. "Good man," she said as she made her way onto the next desk. But before she reached Tracy, an excited DS Fox called her over.

"John, what's up?"

His eyes were bulging out of his ageing face. If he hadn't looked so serious, she would've laughed at his expression. He looked like a fish gasping for air.

"Ma'am, there's been another one." John slumped back in his chair as if voicing the words had sapped all his strength.

"Sorry? Another what exactly, John?" She perched on his desk and folded her arms.

"Another robbery. It happened last night, the same time as the Kellys' crime was being committed."

"What? Jeez! Is it the same MO? Anyone hurt?" Her heart sank as the thought of dealing with another grieving family entered her head.

Recovering his composure John sat forward and picked up his pad. "Nope, doesn't appear to be. It's another footballer, but from a different team."

"Hmm... Which team?"

"Sharlston. Do you think this could be the same gang, ma'am?"

She sighed, taking the pad from his hand she tried to decipher his scrawl. According to his notes, Stacy Kendrickson had been alone with her two kids while husband, footballer Paul Kendrickson, was involved in a match. When he arrived home at approximately eleven p.m., he found his wife lying in the lounge, her hands tied behind her back. Their two children were asleep upstairs in their beds. *Thank God for that!*

"Fancy a trip out there, John? Take Molly with you, will you? The experience will be good for her."

John shot out of his chair and slipped his black jacket over his blue shirt. "Will do, ma'am. We shouldn't be long."

"Be as long as you need to be. Have patience when you're questioning the husband and wife. There's no rush. Umm... Get Molly to ask the wife if she was assaulted at all. Ask her if she'd be willing to come in for a line-up if the need arises."

"Yes, ma'am. Molly, grab your coat. You're coming with me."

At first Molly appeared shocked that she was being set free from the office, but then she hurriedly pulled on her jacket and hoisted her handbag over her shoulder and tucked her chair under the desk.

"I'm ready," she announced, and Lorne had to suppress a chuckle.

Lorne bid the two detectives farewell and made her way over to Katy's desk. "Just checking: You'll be okay with the security firm?"

Katy gave a stern nod, picked up the sheet of paper with the address of the firm on it, and headed for the door. "I'll be a couple of hours, I guess, provided the Sat Nav doesn't get me lost," she called over her shoulder as she exited the incident room.

Lorne continued round the room. Tracy, the young sergeant who had shown so much initiative in Lorne's last term as DI, was on the phone, urgently scribbling down and adding information to an already extensive list.

"Damn," Lorne said, shaking her head.

"Ma'am?" Tracy queried.

"Contact DS Fox on his mobile, will you, Tracy? I forgot to tell him to take pictures of the scene. Let's hope he's got a camera on that antiquated phone of his."

Tracy giggled. "Oh, he has, ma'am. I saw the guys comparing photos the other day."

Frowning and intrigued, she asked, "Oh, do tell?"

The young sergeant's cheeks flushed when she realised what she'd told her superior. "Hmm... Maybe I shouldn't have said anything, ma'am."

"Maybe I'll ask the guys to show me the next time we go to the pub; should make for an entertaining half-hour or so. In the meantime, after you've rung John, can you get the number for the director of Borthwick City for me?"

"Ma'am, I'll put it through to your office."

"Okay, then ring this number. It's Mrs. Kelly's best friend. She should've sat with Mrs. Kelly last night but couldn't make it. Let her know what happened, will you? Also ask her if she knows the name of the designer the Kellys used."

"Yes, ma'am."

Lorne stopped at the coffee machine outside her office, inserted fifty pence into the slot, and selected a strong black coffee.

The phone on her desk rang the second she stepped inside her office. She answered it.

"Ma'am, I've got the director on the line for you. Her name is Deb Brownlee."

"Thanks, Tracy." Lorne heard a click and then someone breathing heavily on the line. "Ms. Brownlee?"

"It is, Inspector. What can I help you with?"

The woman's tone sounded a little off to Lorne's ear. She cautiously continued, "Ms. Brownlee, first of all, can you tell me why the footballers weren't told to up their security, in light of what happened to the Dobbs family?"

After a slight pause the woman responded, "Was there really a necessity for that?"

Lorne's lips pulled into a straight line, and she could feel her blood heat up in her veins. Covering the mouthpiece to the phone, she blew out a breath, then uncovered it again. "You are aware of what happened at the Kellys' home last night, aren't you?"

"Yes," the woman said abruptly.

"So I take it you'll be making the other footballers at your club aware of the situation and ensuring they up their security, at least for the time being?"

"Inspector, what the footballers get up to when they're away from this club is up to them. We don't treat our staff like children."

Lorne glared out the window and pictured the woman on the other end of the line, no doubt dressed in a designer suit, with pristine manicured fingernails and her hair shaped and coiffed by an exclusive hair stylist in Oxford Street.

"I understand that, Ms. Brownlee. But as with any business, I'd expect work colleagues to be aware of the dangers surrounding them. Especially as this is the second *serious* crime of this nature to have happened within the last forty-eight hours."

"Things happen."

Which to Lorne sounded like the phrase 'Shit happens.' "Okay, I'm not sure where you're coming from on this issue, Ms. Brownlee, but I'm *officially* asking you to make sure the other footballers are aware of this situation and to make sure they get adequate security until the criminals are apprehended."

"Officially? You mean you can *make* people obtain extra security?"

The snootiness in the woman's voice and her attitude made Lorne shudder. The woman had Lorne by the short and curlies.

"What harm can it do?" Lorne snapped back at her.

"I'm a busy person, Inspector. If that's all... I'll be going now." And with that bumptious retort, Ms. Brownlee hung up.

Lorne made a note on her pad to call back and give the heartless woman a piece of her mind when there was a lull in the case.

Tracy entered the room and gave Lorne a sheet of paper with the name of the Kellys' designer: Danielle Styles of Styles Interiors. Lorne added the sheet to her growing to-do pile.

* * *

A few hours later, John and Molly returned from the Kendricksons' home at the same time Katy stormed through the door. Lorne pondered whom to tackle first, but after noticing the way Katy's mouth was twitching in anger, she thought that John and Molly would be quicker to get out of the way. "John, what did you learn? Did you get the photos?"

He handed her his phone, and she scrolled through the pictures. She quickly found what she'd been expecting. "As I thought, the furnishings are different from the other properties."

"Ma'am?" John queried.

"With that in mind, I think we're looking at a totally different gang. With the first two houses, the décors were the same. Do we know what security firm the Kendricksons used?"

"Hang on a mo. I wrote it down here somewhere."

Molly tutted and told her, "It's 'Trust Us,' ma'am."

"Hmm… That's interesting. It's the same firm as the other families. And yet the décor is different. I'll need to check into this further before making any assumptions." But her gut instinct, the thing she'd always relied heavily upon, was telling her that there was something dodgy about the security firm.

Speaking of which, she walked over to Katy's desk and perched on the edge of the desk beside it. "Katy?"

"Ma'am?" she replied pensively.

"How did it go? With the security firm, I mean."

Katy threw her pen across her desk. "Jumped-up little prick wouldn't tell me anything. Get a warrant, he said."

"I see, and your response to that was?"

Katy gave her a quizzical look and shrugged. "I left. What else could I do?"

"I see. Well, maybe we'll both go and see them tomorrow."

Katy's frown turned into a scowl. "With a warrant?"

"Not necessary, DS Foster. You'll see." Lorne winked.

Lorne smiled, turned, and headed back to her office, but heard the new recruit mutter, "Good luck on that one; you're gonna need it."

51

By the time seven o'clock came around, Lorne had a stinking headache and decided to call it a day. She drove back home in a daze, her thoughts caught up in the complexities of the case and worrying if Tony had arrived safely in Afghanistan.

As usual, Henry met her at the front door, whined, and bolted to the back door to be let out.

"All right, boy. Busting are you?" She ruffled his head and unlocked the back door to let him out.

After putting on the kettle and searching for her painkillers in the cupboard, she walked into the lounge to see if there were any messages on the phone. Disappointed, she returned to the kitchen and let Henry in.

"Now, what shall we have for dinner?"

Henry barked and started leaping around. Despite the pain in her head, she found herself laughing at his antics.

Looking through the fridge, she found some leftover chicken she'd set aside for him. Adding his quota of biscuits for the day to the dish, she put it on the floor. The dog pounced on it as if he'd been starved for a couple of weeks.

"Hey, slow down. You'll get an ulcer!"

Returning to the fridge, she explored what else was lurking within its depths and came out with the usual ingredients for a quick meal: eggs, tomatoes, cheese, and bacon. Taking a frying pan from the cupboard, she rustled up an omelette on the stove before flashing it under the grill to fluff up.

At the table, she ate her omelette with one hand while she lazily stroked the dog sitting beside her, waiting in hope for any leftovers.

The phone rang just as she popped the last mouthful in her mouth. Swallowing her food, she answered. "Tony?"

"Sorry, love, it's me," her father said quietly. "Not heard from him yet, then, I take it?"

She expelled a long breath and slumped into the leather sofa. "Hi, Dad. No, I haven't heard from him yet. He'll probably ring tonight."

"Probably, love. What's it like being back in the rat race?"

Lorne switched the TV to the BBC news. "You know, busy. Working a crappy case at the moment that's frustrating me, but then, what's new?"

Her father remained silent for a few seconds before asking, "Anything I can help you with?"

Sam Collins had been a DCI in the Met, but retired over seven years ago. He was one of the old-school coppers, the kind who relied on gut instinct and brainpower to solve their cases. With all the different kinds of modern forensics in place, a lot of the guesswork and detective skills had been taken out of police work. That was one of the reasons he'd welcomed his retirement when it had arrived.

"Not really, Dad. The case will be all over the news soon enough, so I might as well tell you. We've had a couple of burglaries in the Chelsea area lately. When I say *burglaries*, there've also been a few fatalities involved, too. That's why my team's been called in."

"I see, and you think there might be a connection, love?"

"Looks like it, although another burglary was reported last night, and everything points to a copycat case for that one." Lorne flicked through a *Home and Gardens* magazine on the table in front of her.

"What makes you think that?"

"All three cases are linked insofar as the victims are footballers. The first two, the victim's kids were killed, and the wives were violently attacked."

"Oh, my God, that's awful. What's different about the third case, Lorne?"

She sighed. "The wife was tied up and the kids were left alone in their beds."

"Hmm… Was the victim married to a footballer, though?"

"Yes, Dad."

"When did the first case happen?" her father asked.

"The night before last," she said, pushing the magazine to one side.

"And the second case?"

"Last night," she replied, wondering where he was going with the line of questions.

"And the third case?"

"That was last night, too. What are you getting at, Dad?" She massaged her temple, hoping to shift the pain that had settled there.

"You say you reckon the third case is a copycat case?"

"That's right."

"Think about it, girl. How can it be a copycat case when the details haven't come out in the press yet?"

"Jesus, you're right. I never thought of that. Do you think this could be just a coincidence, then, Dad?"

"Hmm… I'll get back to you on that one. Let me mull things over for a while. Have you rung Charlie today?"

"No, why? Is something wrong?"

Her father laughed, and it sounded good. He didn't really smile or laugh a lot since they'd lost her mother to breast cancer a couple of years before.

"Nothing wrong, love. She rang me tonight to say how excited she was about the weekend ahead. Going ice-skating, aren't you?"

"That's the plan. That reminds me—any chance you can look after Henry for the day? I wanted to spend the whole day with Charlie. You know, take her ice-skating and then stay in town for a meal. Please, Dad?" She knew her father would kick up a fuss, but she also knew that it wouldn't last long, because deep down he loved the dog as if he were his own.

He exhaled, pretending to be mad at the request. "If I must."

Pushing her luck, she added, "Can I pick him up on Sunday morning?"

"Only because I love my granddaughter so much and think she needs to spend more time with her mother. Umm… That'd be you!"

"I get your point, Dad. You're a gem. What about coming to Sunday lunch? Maybe you can bring him back then. I'll do your favourite: roast pork with all the trimmings," she added, trying to appease him.

"Hmm… You certainly know how to get around me, young lady."

"I'll see you Saturday, then, Dad. Love you."

"You take care, sweetie. I'll give your case some thought. If I come up with anything, I'll give you a ring."

"Okay. The minute I hear from Tony, I'll let you know."

Chapter Eleven

Lack of sleep made her eyes hurt, and the next morning, she found it a strain to concentrate on the road ahead. Thick fog and the glare from the car in front's fog lamps added to her difficulty.

Worry was taking a chunk out of her heart, too. Despite all his assurances that he would, Tony had neglected to call the previous evening. He *always* made sure he found time in his busy schedule to call her. Which meant one of two things: Either he had arrived at his destination and it was way out of reach of any communication posts, or he'd been captured by the Taliban. She was hoping it was the former of the two scenarios. It didn't stop that niggling gut instinct she relied upon so much to start up.

He's fine. Now where will worrying unnecessarily get you?

She nodded as if answering herself and indicated right at the next traffic lights. Parking the car in the station car park, she sucked in a few breaths and began her working day.

Most of the team was already at their desks when she arrived. "All quiet last night, AJ?"

"Appears to be so far, ma'am."

"That's a relief. I'll be in my office if you need me. Is Katy here yet?" Lorne asked, searching the room.

"Not yet, ma'am…"

They both glanced up at the clock. Eight fifty-five. She still had five minutes to make it.

"Send her in when she gets here, will you?"

"Will do," AJ replied.

Lorne started on the mail lying on her desk and soon spotted the pathology reports from Patti. There it was in black and white: no evidence to go on. The kids were killed, and their mothers beaten, but not a single hair or fingerprint was picked up to help their case. She opened the rest of the post, feeling disheartened by the news. *Bloody paperwork!*

Half an hour had flown past before she realised there was still no sign of Katy. She kicked out at the table leg in annoyance. *Great! I wanted to get down to the security firm first thing.*

Lorne left her office to find out what was going on. She called across the incident room, "AJ, no Katy, yet?"

An uncomfortable look covered his handsome face, and he avoided eye contact with her. She knew there was something wrong even before he opened his mouth.

"She arrived about five minutes ago, ma'am. Umm… She's in the ladies'."

Without responding, Lorne headed for the loo, fearing what she was going to find, if AJ's demeanour was anything to go by.

At first the toilet appeared to be empty, but then Lorne saw that one of the cubicles was occupied. "Katy? You in there?"

"Shit."

Lorne heard a fair amount of shuffling coming from inside the loo. "Are you coming out?" she prompted gently.

Silence filled the cold, echoing room. Sighing heavily, Lorne tried again, her patience waning. "I said, 'Are you—'"

The bolt sounded on the door, and it eased open. The left side of her face showing in the gap, Katy said, "Sorry ma'am. I've been sick. Thought I'd be all right for work, but…"

Something told Lorne that her sergeant wasn't telling her the truth. She stepped up to the cubicle and pushed the door back. "Oh my God! What the hell happened to you?"

Ashamed, Katy's head dropped. She walked past Lorne and over to the sink. Resting her hands on the porcelain sink, she raised her head up to the cracked mirror above.

Lorne patiently waited for the sergeant to tell her why she had a black eye, a beauty at that. When she sensed no response was imminent, she placed her hand on the younger woman's arm.

Katy flinched and stepped sideways.

"Katy, it's all right. Come on. Tell me who did it?"

"I can't," Katy mumbled.

"Why on earth not? Were you mugged? Didn't you see your attacker? Did they come at you from behind?"

With each question, the sergeant shook her head, which only caused Lorne to be more confused. She might've been an excellent detective, but her psychic skills were in serious doubt.

Softly, she asked, "Was it someone you know, Katy?"

The sergeant's gaze remained focused on the floor in front of her, and Lorne suspected she'd just given herself the answer.

"Do you want to press charges, love?" Memories of her own abusive marriage to Tom made her reach out to the young sergeant. She knew what it was like to live a lie, to pretend to those around you that everything was hunky-dory at home, when nothing was further from the truth. At least she'd had the foresight and courage to get out of her marriage before it had escalated to anything as bad as what Katy was obviously going through.

"I couldn't," the sergeant said, eventually finding her voice.

"Why?"

"I just can't. It was my fault," Katy said, avoiding eye contact with Lorne.

Lorne exhaled a deep breath. How many times had she heard that over the years when dealing with abused wives or girlfriends? Too many. The abused always blamed themselves, believing what their abusive partners had told them during their beatings, often having to deal with numerous violent beatings that in the worst cases left the woman hospitalized, sometimes fighting for her life on a ventilator.

"Nothing you could've done would warrant a beating like that, love. Nothing. Come on, talk to me." She tried to give the younger woman a smile to reassure her, but Katy's vision remained glued to the ground.

"I can't," she repeated. Her right foot made a circle on the tiled floor in front of her.

"Okay. You know what I told you about my door always being open? That still stands."

"Thanks, I appreciate that, but I'll be fine. I can deal with it."

Lorne slammed her hip against the sink and folded her arms. "You don't look 'fine.' I'd suggest you take the day off, but on second thought, I think I'd probably be sending you back home for another beating. Did your boyfriend do this?"

Continuing to toe the floor, Katy gave a brief but reluctant nod.

"Does he make a habit of doing this?"

"This is the second time."

"Is that why you were transferred?" Lorne asked as the mystery behind why the new sergeant had moved slotted into place. Did Sean Roberts know about her background? Did the super come to that conclusion too? Had they transferred her for her own safety, since she was unwilling to press charges against the bastard?

Katy shrugged, neither confirming nor denying in response.

"What do you want to do, Katy?"

"Ma'am?" she replied, her eyes finally meeting Lorne's.

"Is he at your place?"

"Yes."

Lorne smiled and patted her arm. "Well, you can't go back there, then. What about staying with me for a few days?"

"I couldn't." She looked shocked at the prospect.

"Why not? Give me one good reason." Lorne watched Katy scrape her foot back and forward on the floor a few more times before adding, "That's settled. After work, we'll drop by your place, and you can pack a few things. It'll be fun, and I can get to know you a little better. Actually, it'll be like old times. Pete often stayed over."

Lorne watched the different faces Katy pulled, something akin to relief and cringing all rolled into one.

In the end, Katy gave a defeated shrug.

"You stay here. I'll go get you some camouflage." Lorne walked through the incident room and into her office. She pulled out an old tube of foundation from deep inside her handbag. The top was caked and hard to shift at first, but after a few seconds, she succeeded in opening it. After wiping the top, she squeezed a little out to test that it hadn't separated too much.

Then Lorne retraced her steps through the group, pausing at Tracy's desk. The young officer looked concerned.

Lorne patted Tracy on the shoulder. "It's all right. She'll be fine. Katy will be staying with me for a couple of days."

"I was going to offer to put her up, ma'am." Tracy looked relieved.

Lorne suspected her relief was more out of concern for Katy than not wanting to become involved in a relationship dispute. "I'm sure she would've appreciated that. I'd like to get to know her a bit more, and with Tony being away, this works out well for both of us."

"Ma'am?"

"Tony's had to go away for a few days on an internal course," Lorne lied, regretting that she had mentioned he'd been called away.

"I see. If there is anything I can do, don't hesitate to ask, ma'am."

"I'll let Katy know you're concerned about her." Lorne pushed open the door to the ladies' and found Katy staring in the mirror, a wad of toilet paper in her hand, dabbing at her black eye.

"Here. Let me see." She gripped Katy by the shoulders and gently wiped the area dry with a tissue before she tentatively started applying the makeup. She covered the affected area with three layers. It wasn't perfect by any stretch of the imagination, because of their different skin tones, but it was a darn sight better than the rainbow colours Katy had walked into work with, not half an hour before.

The exercise had shown how tough Katy was. She flinched once or twice when Lorne had blended the makeup, but overall, her shoulders had been pulled back with determination, and she'd put up with the pain inflicted, taking it in her stride.

"There. A certain part of you might look like a clown, but I'm sure people won't stop and stare at you now."

Katy turned to survey Lorne's artistic flair and nodded her approval. "Maybe you missed your vocation, ma'am."

Lorne smiled. "You fit and willing to start duty now, Sergeant?"

Standing to attention, Katy mock saluted and made for the door.

"Right, let's go and pay this friendly security firm a visit, shall we?"

Chapter Twelve

They arrived at the swanky office of Trust Us at just after ten. The office was in the middle of a trading estate on the outskirts of East Finchley. The place, which looked more like a showroom than any security office Lorne had ever been in, was decorated in slate grey, and all the furniture was either chrome or black. Two of the four desks were occupied by young, suited men who obviously earned enough not to buy off-the-rack suits.

As soon as the two detectives walked into the office, one of the men gave them a guarded look. He stepped from behind his desk at the rear of the office and approached them, his arm extended ready to shake hands. Lorne deliberately ignored his hand and reached into her pocket to pull out her ID. It was her intention to make the guy feel uneasy from the start.

"I'm DI Simpkins, and this is my partner DS Foster. Show the nice man your ID, will you? Oh no, don't bother. He's already seen yours once, hasn't he?"

Katy had told Lorne outside that he was the guy who'd blatantly refused to give her any of the details she had asked for the previous day, and Lorne was now gunning for him.

The man's face dropped along with his outstretched arm, and he had the decency to look slightly embarrassed. "I… umm…"

Lorne turned her head sideways and held her ear out to the man. "Come on, Mr.…? I'm dying to hear why you tried to obstruct a case yesterday. For your information, judges don't take kindly to that kind of thing in a court of law."

The man's jaw flew open, and his demeanour was one of discomfort under her glare. "It's Philip Underhill. Umm… about yesterday. Er… I can explain."

"I'm waiting," she said, her eyebrows disappearing under her fringe.

"I was about to go out when… your partner arrived. I had an urgent appointment that I couldn't be late for. An important client. You know how it is."

"Actually, I don't. My partner was trying to ascertain important information that could make or break our case. In all my years on the force, I've never had to obtain a warrant to gain a client's details from a security firm before. Why the heck should your firm be any different? Answer me that, Mr. Underhill."

The six-foot-two, mousey-haired guy stuttered as he apologized. "I—I'm sorry... You're right, Inspector." Turning to Katy, he smiled, though it was more like a grimace. "It was rude and unforgivable of me."

"At least we're agreed on one thing. Now, if you have the time, I'd like to see the files you have for the Dobbses and the Kellys."

He moved towards the black filing cabinet nearest his desk, and after taking a key from his waistcoat pocket, unlocked it.

"Let me see. Ahh, here's one." He took a manila folder out of the top drawer and placed it on his desk.

Lorne wandered over and picked up the file and began to read through it. Katy joined her and took the other file from Underhill's hand before he had a chance to place it on his clutter-free desk.

"What sort of operation do you run here?" Lorne asked, looking up from the file and glancing round the office. "I've never seen a security firm with such plush office space before, and I didn't see any kind of warehouse attached."

Yes, the building was on an industrial estate, but she had expected some kind of storage unit or factory-type setup. She had her doubts about whether he'd offer her the truth.

"We decided to split the locations. Our warehouse is on the other side of London."

Lorne frowned. "Why? That doesn't seem a very practical situation."

With an air of cockiness he responded, "It suits us. Our systems are second to none. Highly rel—" His cheeks reddened when he realized his mistake.

"Go on. I think you were about to assure us how highly reliable your systems are and your firm is, am I right?"

Underhill fidgeted on the spot for a few seconds before he propped his backside on the desk, tucking his hands between his thighs. "All right. I confess, maybe our systems have been a little dodgy lately, but..."

Sensing he was about to come out with some form of bullshit or other, Lorne raised her hand to stop him. "A *little* dodgy. No shit, Sherlock. And because of your systems conveniently failing like that, we've now got three dead kids lying in our mortuary fridges."

If Lorne didn't know any better, she would've said that snippet of information was news to him as the colour drained from his scrawny face.

"You weren't aware of that fact, Mr. Underhill?" she queried.

He sighed heavily. "No, I wasn't aware of that, Inspector. I'm deeply sorry."

She gave a brief nod. "I'll be sure to pass on your condolences to the families concerned. What I want and need to know is why your super-duper systems failed. Twice on consecutive days?"

His sagging shoulders pulled upright and a puzzled look appeared on his face. "Are you implying something, Inspector?"

He was a smart cookie despite looking wet behind the ears and a regular mummy's boy, but Lorne was smarter despite her two-year absence from the force.

"Should I be? Is there something you want to tell me?" She looked over her shoulder, then back at him and leaned in. "In private, if you'd rather."

Underhill didn't appreciate her invading his personal space and edged back a little. "I have nothing to hide, Inspector. The system failed. It's as simple as that."

Lorne was intentionally quiet for the next couple of minutes while she looked through the file. It was a trick her father had taught her when she had first joined the force. A sure way to unnerve someone was to give them enough rope to hang themselves with, then to pull back and see how they reacted.

"So my understanding is… Hold on. Before I ask that, is there a report for the breakdown yet?"

"Not yet," he snapped back.

"Okay, here's how I see it, Mr. Underhill. First of all, I think it's shoddy, very shoddy, that you haven't got a report yet. And second, I find it totally inconceivable to think on two separate occasions your systems *conveniently* malfunctioned. Furthermore, that the two—no, three—crimes all involved footballers."

"Now wait just a fucking minute." Underhill rose to his feet and stepped forward, trying to intimidate Lorne.

She stood her ground and glared at him. "Language, Mr. Underhill. I see you don't seem to have much respect for either women or the law." Lorne turned to face Katy and winked. "We don't take kindly to disrespecting the law, do we, Sergeant? What say we take this down the station?" She turned back to Underhill and suppressed a smile. "Ever been hauled in for questioning before? We'll even give you the thrill of putting the siren on, if you like."

He reached for the mobile sitting on his paper-free desk. "We'll see what my solicitor thinks about that, shall we?"

Lorne shrugged. "You know that's the first sign of guilt, don't you? If you have nothing to hide, why would you want to consult your solicitor?"

He forced out a long breath and flicked his mobile across his desk. Looking at his watch, he told her, "I've got a client to see in half an hour. What do you want to know, Inspector?"

"I want to see your breakdown reports for the last two years."

Underhill's mouth dropped open again, and his colleague, who up till then had remained quiet, sniggered.

The colleague's smugness infuriated Lorne. She shot him a dirty look and moved to stand in front of his desk. "Something funny about that?"

He laughed again and said, "Our records only go back to the beginning of the year."

She sharply turned back to Underhill. "Is that true?" When he nodded, she added, "Why?"

"We're a new business."

"How did you manage to get such high-profile clients then?"

He shrugged. "Lucky break. I was in the right place at the right time and overheard someone talking in a pub. The rest, as they say, is history!"

"Do you have a name for this *someone*?" Lorne asked, thinking that she was finally getting somewhere.

"Umm… let me think."

She sensed he was stalling for time and turned back to the squirt sitting behind the desk. "His name?"

Gulping at the harshness in her tone, the man mumbled, "It was Zac something or other."

He refused to make eye contact with her, so she took that to mean he was being economical with the truth. Baring her teeth in a false smile, she prompted, "Try harder."

It was Underhill who spoke next. "That's all I know him as, Zac."

"All right, which pub?"

"The Cross Keys, just down the road."

Lorne nodded at Katy to note it down in her notebook. "Is he a regular?"

Underhill's mouth turned down. "He said he was. Seemed pretty friendly with the busty barmaid."

Both men laughed, and Lorne shook her head in disgust. If the men thought they had managed to divert Lorne's attention from them, they had another think coming. "I'd still like to see your reports."

That wiped the smile off Underhill's face. He went back to the filing cabinet, and that time, he searched the second drawer down. "There you go. I told you there weren't many."

Lorne opened the file and was surprised to find it empty. "You're kidding me?"

Underhill shook his head and shrugged. "Nope. I told you... our systems are shit hot."

"Which leaves me wondering why these families had break-ins on consecutive nights in an otherwise fault-free system. Oh, and before you say it, I ain't really one for coincidences, Mr. Underhill."

He shrugged. Lorne decided to let him stew on her words and headed for the door. "You don't mind if we take these files with us, do you?" She raised her eyes to the ceiling and blew out an exasperated breath. "Let's hope we don't have any more incidences of mysterious breakdowns for the rest of the week, for your sake."

For the first time, she'd rendered the young man speechless. He merely nodded his agreement for her to take the files and moved behind his desk to sit down.

The two detectives left before he regained his composure again. They got back in the car and all of a sudden Katy roared with laughter.

Confused by her outburst, Lorne asked, "Something wrong?"

When Katy had calmed down, she replied, "You don't take any prisoners, do you?"

Lorne smiled and started the car. "Ah, you've noticed that. Trouble is, I can't stand cockiness. The little prick was trying to pull the wool over our eyes because we're women. Unfortunately, I've come across thousands of his sort over the years. I get a thrill putting his type down."

Twenty minutes later, Lorne pulled up outside the baker's close to the station where, back in the good old days, Pete and she used to buy their lunches.

Katy went inside and returned carrying three cake boxes and a carrier bag.

Shaking her head in disbelief, Lorne said, "Jeez, you didn't have to buy the whole shop. I only wanted a sandwich."

Katy smiled, and for the first time, Lorne noticed the sergeant's beautifully white teeth that had obviously been touched up by her dentist and the cute dimple in her left cheek. "Thought I'd treat the team to a chocolate éclair. Everyone loves an éclair, don't they?"

"You know what, I think you're gonna fit in just fine, DS Foster. Oh, and as I'm the senior officer, the biggest éclair *always* comes my way."

Chapter Thirteen

"Everything all right, Bro?" His brother shuffled from one foot to the other and avoided eye contact with him. "Come on. What's eating you?"

Zac sat down at the island in the kitchen of his brother's old but beautifully restored manor house. "Not sure how to tell you this," Zac said hesitantly.

He sat down opposite and tipped his brother's face up to meet his. "Just say it."

"While we were on the job the other night, word has it that another house was being hit at the same time."

He frowned and folded his arms across his broad chest. "What's so strange about that? Do you know how many break-ins there are in London every year?"

"You're missin' the point, Bro. Another footballer got hit. You know, like we're doin'."

The boss man leaned his elbows on the worktop and thought about the scenario for a second or two before responding. Another robbery, focusing on *their* target victims. *Hmmm...* He didn't like the sound of that. His heart started to pump the blood round his veins harder and faster, and he was sure his cheeks had gone red.

He jumped off the stool, and it tipped to the floor behind him. "How the fuck did that happen? What else do you know?"

Zac's hand trembled and clenched shut. "It's all a bit sketchy. That's all I know at the mo, Bro."

"What plans have you got today? It doesn't matter. Cancel them and get down the pub. Ask around a bit; see what you can find out. I wanna know who's behind it, you hear me?"

Zac jumped off the stool and left the room faster than a racing greyhound. After his brother slammed the back door shut behind him, he picked up his mobile.

He had two calls to make, and he drummed impatient fingers on the granite worktop in front of him while waiting for his first contact to pick up.

"It's me. You told me they were loaded. That was bullshit. I ain't risking my life again for some piddly bits of costume jewellery, you hear me? Next time, get your facts right... Yeah, killing the kids was unfortunate, but the women wound me up. Be in touch soon."

He hung up and was starting to get doubts about being involved with this hare-brained scheme. One more job the following week, and they'd have to call it a day. He placed his second call. "Stan?"

"Is that you?" the rough voice asked.

"Yeah, it's me. You fenced that gear yet?"

"Give us a break, man. It's only been a couple of days," Stan replied nervously.

"Well… What the fuck are you playing at? Get it out of the country pronto."

"Why? What's going on?"

"Just do it. Don't ask stupid questions. Get back to me later when you've got shot of it. *Today*, got it?"

"Yep, reading you loud and clear; but if it goes abroad, it ain't gonna fetch the money it would here."

"I don't care, just get *rid*." He disconnected the phone and started pacing the room. He hated it when his plans went to pot. Fair enough if he'd been the one to screw up, but he hated it even more when the fault lay at someone else's door. Now he'd have to sit around and wait. Wait for the gear to be sold and wait for word from his brother. He wasn't good at waiting patiently. "Rex, come 'ere."

The doc-tailed Rottweiler trotted into the kitchen and nuzzled at his hand. "Get your lead, son. We're going for a long walk."

The dog ran into the hallway and appeared moments later with his lead hanging from his mouth, slobber hitting the Travertine tiles below.

It was time to clear his head and do some deep thinking. If someone was out to make trouble for him, he'd need his wits about him to outsmart them. A brisk stroll down by the canal with his monster of a dog usually did the trick. He smiled at the thought of the dog tearing one of the ducks to pieces like he usually did. *Nothing like a bit of blood and guts to brighten one's day.*

* * *

After the team had finished their lunches, Lorne took a spare éclair through to DCI Roberts. He eyed it suspiciously as though he was expecting it to explode any second and plaster the walls of his office with cream and chocolate.

Lorne laughed and explained, "It's a treat from Katy." She winked and pointed to the small bulge overhanging his belt that showed prominently while he sat behind his desk. He sucked his stomach in and glared at her. Leaning forward, she whispered behind her hand. "Hey, I promise not to tell your wife."

He motioned for her to sit opposite him and asked, "How is Foster settling in?"

She detected wariness in his tone. Sitting down, she said, "I think she's already shaping up to be a good team member." Okay, it was a bit of a fib. Foster still had a long way to go before she would class her as a top partner; but upon reflection, Pete, who she'd always regarded as good, had more than his share of faults. Most of the time, she had chosen to overlook them.

His hands steepled in front of him. "Hmmm… Is that so?"

"Sir?"

"What's this I hear about her coming to work looking like she'd just gone three rounds with Amir Khan, then?"

Lorne wriggled uncomfortably in her chair, and her gaze dropped to the desk in front of her. Oh what the heck, he'd find out soon enough. "It's sorted. She's going to be staying with me for a few days."

One eyebrow cocked, he asked, "Is Tony okay with that?"

"Umm… Tony's on a course for a few days."

"Oh. I didn't know. So how did she get it?" She shrugged, and he prompted, "Lorne? You need to tell me. Supposing Greenfall asks me what happened, what am I going to tell him?"

"Give the girl a break, Sean. It's a personal matter between her and her…"

"What? Her boyfriend did that to her?"

Shit! Me and my big mouth!

Lorne expelled the breath she'd just sucked in and gave a brief nod. "I'm handling it. When we pick up her bag tonight, I'll read him the riot act. He won't lay another hand on her if he knows what's good for him. Answer me this: is that why she was transferred?"

"I have no idea. Maybe it is. Maybe Greenfall and her parents know she's in an abusive relationship. Maybe they thought the distance would be good for them both. My bet is that they hadn't anticipated him following her down south. They'll be livid when or if they find out. What state of mind is she in?"

"She's fine. I'll keep a close eye on her, but she was actually laughing in the car."

"That sounds positive. About what, exactly?"

Lorne filled him in on their trip to the security firm, and he winked at her and gave her a knowing nod. "Another set of balls chewed off, ready to add to your collection, then?"

"Yeah, you know what I'm like with cocksure wimps."

He nodded and appeared to drift off for a moment. Lorne suspected he was recalling when they'd been involved in a relationship, before her marriage to Tom. Their relationship had been verbally volatile most of the time. She'd even called him a 'cocksure wimp' on more than one occasion, she seemed to remember. But their making up had been the best thing about their arguments. Her cheeks reddened as the image fleetingly filtered her mind.

Awkwardly, he cleared his throat and mumbled, "Yes, I remember all too well, Inspector. So, where are we with regard to the case? What's this I hear about a third case? AJ told me you're not tying the case to the other two. Any reason?"

She could tell this was his idea of testing her, to see if she was up to the task in hand. "I have a theory. I suspect it's some kind of copycat case, but Dad doesn't agree."

If she'd been talking to anyone else, her father's name wouldn't have been mentioned, but Sean and Sam Collins went back a long way. His advice had been instrumental in solving the case when Baldwin had kidnapped her daughter Charlie.

"Why doesn't Sam agree?" Sean asked, looking puzzled.

"He has a point, I guess, but he reckons it can't be a copycat case because it hasn't appeared in the media yet."

"What hasn't? I'm not with you."

"And you thought I would be the rusty one? Hmm… The *case* hasn't appeared in the papers. So how could another gang copy it?"

"Ah, I see. Well I'm inclined to agree with him. Did your father have any ideas?"

"He's thinking about it. You know what he's like. He'll plot it out methodically, as he usually does, leaving me to get on with the nitty-gritty of the case. I'll give him a ring tonight and see if he's come up with anything. In the meantime, I'm going to go over the files we brought back from the security firm, see if anything comes to light. You know Trisha Dobbs came out of her coma, don't you?"

"Why do you say it like that? Surely it's a good thing that she's regained consciousness, isn't it?"

Lorne sighed and crossed one leg over the other. "It would be if she could remember anything about that night. Mr. Dobbs is dreading telling his wife their kids were killed."

"I can totally understand his apprehension. Let's hope she successfully regains her memory."

"I'll second that. I'm going to call in on Sandra Kelly on the way to Katy's place later, see if there's any change there."

"Right, I better let you get on, then. Keep me informed."

Lorne stood up and walked toward the door but paused when she heard him say. "I knew I did the right thing asking you to come back."

Under her breath, she replied, "That remains to be seen. I haven't cracked the case yet."

Chapter Fourteen

Lorne and Katy ended their shift at six thirty p.m. and drove to the hospital to check on both the injured wives. Lorne thought it would be silly to drive all that way without checking how both of them were progressing.

Standing outside Sandra Kelly's room, the detectives heard sobbing and raised voices coming from inside the private ward. Lorne knocked and waited. She knocked a second time and eased the door open a little. "All right if we come in?"

Les Kelly stood over by the window, looking out at the car park below, and his wife sat up in bed, sobbing uncontrollably. Sniffling, she reached over and plucked a tissue from the square box on the bedside table. She delicately blew her nose and dried her eyes before asking, "Who are you?"

Her husband left the window and sat in the chair beside her. "This is the detective in charge of the case, Sandy."

Her eyes screwed up, and on another sob, she snapped at Lorne, "Have you caught the bastards who killed my son yet? The ones who did this to me?" Her voice rose into a screech.

Lorne approached the side of the bed and stroked the women's arm. She didn't blame her for lashing out. She would've done the same thing, given the circumstances. "We're doing our best, Mrs. Kelly. Are you up to answering any questions?"

The woman's sobs were punctuated by heavy intakes of breath. "Yes, I suppose so... But it won't bring my baby back, will it?" As soon as she mentioned the word *baby,* tears started to fill and spill from her already red raw eyes.

"I understand your grief, but anything you can tell us about what happened will help us track down the intruders much quicker. We might even be able to prevent it from happening to another family."

Sandra Kelly whipped another tissue from the box and dabbed her eyes dry. Then she pointed to her bandaged head. "As you can see, they pummelled me in the head a few times. It's hard to remember everything."

"I'm sorry. Anything, anything at all, you can think of. For instance, how many men were there, can you remember that?" Lorne asked gently.

The woman was quiet for a few moments. Lorne could tell she was finding it extremely difficult to search her damaged mind. Suddenly, it was like a light bulb had gone off in Sandra's head. Had Lorne's question sparked a memory?

"I remember. There were three of them. I don't think they mentioned anyone outside, but I might be wrong."

"That's brilliant, Sandra. Do you have any idea how long they were with you?" Lorne patted the women's arm, encouraging her to dig deeper into her confused and battered mind.

"I don't know. It seemed like hours, but I can't say for sure."

Desperate to keep the woman's train of thought on the night in question, she asked, "Can you tell me what the men looked like? Young, middle-aged?"

Sandra shook her head and a pained expression wiped away the hopeful one that had settled on her face moments earlier.

"I'm sorry, their faces are blurred. I was so scared for my baby..." She broke down again, and Lorne looked at Les to comfort her.

"No problem, Mrs. Kelly. Just concentrate on getting yourself better, and give me a call if you remember anything, no matter how insignificant it may seem."

Les smiled and nodded, then gathered his wife in his tattooed arms.

Outside the room, Lorne turned to Katy, whose makeup was starting to wear off. "One step forward and two steps backwards, as usual. We'll just pop in to see the Dobbses, then call it a day. How are you holding up?"

"Me? I'm fine. Dying for a glass of wine, though."

Lorne smiled and nodded as they walked up the stairs to the floor above. When they arrived at Mrs. Dobbs' room, all was quiet. Lorne tapped on the door, and it was instantly opened by the patient's husband, Dave.

"Inspector, any news?" His eyes widened in expectation.

Shaking her head, she told him, "Sorry, not yet. I don't suppose your wife's condition has improved, has it?"

"Nope, she can't remember a thing. Not about the incident or our children's deaths." Tears glistened in his eyes, and his head dropped to his chest.

Lorne knew she could offer him a teeny bit of hope, so she filled him in on the snippet of information Mrs. Kelly had just divulged to them and left.

Next stop was Katy's flat, which turned out to be less than half an hour away from Lorne's house in Highbury. They pulled up outside the terraced Victorian house that had a tiny front garden and two front doors in the porch. Katy inserted her key in the red door on the right. Lorne saw her take a few deep breaths and jabbed her gently in the ribs.

"Be strong. I'm here with you. Just remember that."

Katy nodded and entered the front door, with Lorne, acting as reinforcement, close behind her. They could hear music, louder than Lorne would allow her teenage daughter to have on in her house, coming from the room off to the right.

Pointing at the door, Katy mouthed, "Darren's in there."

Just then, as if he'd heard her, the door flew open. A fair-haired man in his early twenties, sporting a snarl, stood in the doorway to what appeared to be the lounge.

"So you're home, are you?" He glared at Lorne and eyed her up and down. "And who's this?"

"Darren, this is my new partner, DI Lorne Simpkins. I'm going to be staying with her for a day or two." Katy's voice trembled slightly.

Lorne challenged the young man with a well-practiced glare of her own. His head turned sharply at Katy, and he took a step toward her. Katy shrunk back from him, and Lorne's fists clenched down by her side. She would bide her time. She knew better than to dive in feet first.

"Go pack your bag, Katy, while Darren and I have a little chat."

"She's not going anywhere. Get my dinner on," he ordered. Again he took another step closer to Katy, but that time Lorne leapt in front of him to block his way.

"Go on, Katy. Why don't we sit down, Darren?" Lorne pushed her way past him, nudging his shoulder with hers as she walked into the lounge.

She heard Katy's footsteps sound in the hallway and Darren grunt when he followed Lorne back into the room. *Phew.* She let out a relieved sigh. Step one had worked. All she had to do was keep his attention for the next ten or fifteen minutes.

"When did you arrive, Darren?"

He grunted again then mumbled, "Yesterday."

Great. Arrives one day and knocks his girlfriend around the minute he lays eyes on her. Nice chap.

"Settling in all right, are you?" Lorne asked as she surveyed the room. Her immediate reaction was that the flat had a fully furnished agreement. She couldn't see Katy owning all the antiquated furnishings. The room was also in desperate need of decoration. Below the picture rail, the bold patterned wallpaper had started to peel away.

Her gaze dropped to the floor. In front of the '80s-looking gas fire was a poor excuse of a rug. It was mostly threadbare and was missing its fringe here and there.

The two-seater sofa's wooden arms were in need of a good polish, and the beige dralon cover looked as if it had never been cleaned. Lorne almost heaved when she saw the amount of stains on it. She shuddered involuntarily. Along one wall was a G-Plan wall-unit similar to the one her parents had throughout her childhood that had ultimately ended up at the tip over twenty years ago.

The man threw himself into the sofa and pointed to the mismatching red-winged easy chair in the corner. "Not really."

"Have you found a job?" Lorne perched herself on the very edge of the chair, hoping she didn't take any of its inhabitants home on the back of her coat.

Curling his lip, he responded, "What the fuck is this, University Challenge? I know you're the old bill, but you can cut the crap with me, lady."

"Why the anger?" Lorne recognised the signs: He was bored, just like Tom had been bored during their marriage. That was why and when her own domestic violence experience had begun. Once Charlie was at secondary school, Tom had tried for years to find a job in the motor trade he'd left to bring up their daughter. It had been a joint decision for him to become a house husband, purely for financial reasons, as her salary was a few grand more than his.

He kicked at the tassels on the edge of the rug. "Who said I'm angry?"

"You mean a calm person would lash out the way you did with Katy?"

His face showed the tiniest glimmer of remorse, but it instantly disappeared when they heard a drawer slam shut in the bedroom. He jumped out of his chair. Lorne was quicker than him and blocked his path again. "Let her come home with me, Darren. Just for a few days, eh?"

He swept his hand through his hair and looked her in the eye. "But I love her. I need her here with me. You don't know what it's like to be cooped up here all day."

Christ, he's been by himself one day, and he's bored already!

Lorne's compassionate side came to the fore. "Why don't you go back up north for a few days? Visit your parents or your mates."

"My parents are *dead.*"

"I'm sorry to hear that. Why don't you stay with friends for a week or so then? It's bound to be tough at the moment for both of you. It's hard for Katy. She's moved areas, workplaces, and had to deal with moving house at the same time. That's three of the most stressful events a person has to deal with in their lifetime, and she's had to do it all within a few days. Plus, she's bound to be worried about you, too. Go back up north, take a break, and come home again when things have settled down, eh?" She watched his mouth move from side to side and his shoulders relax a little as he thought over her proposal.

That was before Katy appeared with her overnight bag. He stormed over, snatched the bag from her hand and threw it back out into the hallway. Katy looked at Lorne with pure fear in her eyes.

Lorne realised she'd have to start issuing him a warning. She yanked his arm and turned him to face her. "Calm down, Darren. We're going to leave now. Do as I suggest, and go away for a few days."

If she didn't know any better, she could've sworn she saw steam coming out of his ears and nostrils like a raging bull.

"She's not going anywhere, *lady.* Now get the fuck out of my flat."

They held each other's stare for a few seconds before Lorne attempted to make him see reason again. "Last chance, Darren. Katy, go wait in the car."

Katy turned toward the front door, but Darren was quick. He jumped on her back and forced her to the ground. Lorne reached into her handbag to retrieve her cuffs. With her knee in his back, she cuffed one arm and grabbed at his other, which was flailing around. All three of them were either screaming or shouting to be heard.

"You're not doing yourself any favours, Darren. Give it up now, and Katy won't press charges. If you don't, she'll be forced to file a complaint for GBH."

That grabbed his attention. The hallway fell silent. Darren pushed down on Katy and used her body as leverage to stand up. Standing virtually with his nose against Lorne's, he eyed the cuff on his left wrist. "Okay, you win. Get it off me."

"I'll take this off once Katy is in the car."

Katy got to her feet, picked up her bag and apologized to Darren before she went out into the street. Lorne heard the car door slam before she undid the cuffs.

"What a lovely girl she is. You don't deserve her. Why the hell she felt the need to apologise to you, I'll never know. If I ever hear you've laid a hand on her again, I'll haul your arse in a cell quicker than you can say 'I want my solicitor.' You hear me?"

He nodded, and anger pulled his mouth into a taut line.

"Good. If Katy wants to come home, I'll bring her back in a few days. I did say *if.*"

Chapter Fifteen

The car on the drive back was filled with deep sighs and heavy breathing but no talking. Lorne had called ahead and ordered Chinese from her favourite take-away and had just pulled up to collect it. There was no need to stop at the off-licence, as she had a couple of bottles of untouched Chardonnay in the fridge at home.

"Oh, just one thing," Lorne said as they walked up the path to her home. "I hope you like dogs. I've got a collie. He's a tad skittish. He'll take some time to get used to you. I ask all my visitors not to make eye contact with him. He'll come round eventually. I think he's just over-protective; it's either that or jealousy, we're not sure which. He doesn't tend to like men much, takes him longer to get used to them for some reason." She laughed, trying to break the tension that had developed since they'd left her flat.

"Maybe we should all avoid men altogether, might solve a lot of issues," Katy mumbled, hunkering down into her coat as a gust of wind rose up.

"A couple of years ago, I might've agreed with that statement. But Tony is a real gem. I'm lucky to have him—when he's around, that is."

Lorne placed the key in the lock and heard the patter of paws coming up the hallway. "Remember what I said: no eye contact. Hi, hon, have you been a good boy?"

Henry's usual routine was to bolt for the back door to be let out. Instead, he ignored Lorne's outstretched hand and went straight up to Katy. He sniffed the hem of her coat and worked his way up it. Her hands were down by her side, and when he reached her right hand, he licked it.

Lorne was shocked and surprised. She nodded for Katy to pet him. Katy stroked round Henry's ear. His tail wagged, then he ran back down the hallway through the kitchen and barked to be let out at the back door.

"He's the demanding male in this house," she said, laughing. "Wow, you're honoured. He's never greeted anyone like that before. It took him months to get used to Tony." Lorne followed the dog into the kitchen.

Katy smiled, shrugged out of her coat, and hung it up with the others on the rack by the front door. "My parents have always had dogs. I think they sense when people have an affinity for them."

"Come through to the kitchen. I'll plate up, if you can open the wine for me?"

When she let Henry back in, he went straight over and sat in front of Katy, expecting to be made a fuss of, totally ignoring the evening meal that Lorne had prepared. The whole scenario made Lorne realise that her immediate reservations about Katy were unjustified. Henry was a good judge of character, after all.

She put the plate of sweet-and-sour pork with egg fried rice down in front of Katy. "Looks like you've got a friend for life there."

"He's a sweetheart. Thanks for today, boss," Katy said, to Lorne's surprise.

"For a start, it's Lorne when we're either off-duty or by ourselves. And second, I take care of my partners. I'm not saying we'll ever have a strong partnership to match the one I had with Pete, but we can try, eh?"

"Can I ask what happened to him?" Katy asked, tentatively putting a forkful of rice into her mouth.

"My nemesis, The Unicorn, killed him. He led us into a trap and pinned us down in an alley." Lorne swallowed noisily, and her misted-up eyes dropped to her half-eaten plate of food. "I never want that to happen again."

"There's no guarantee in this job, Lorne. We could be led into a trap every day. Seems to me that criminals are getting smarter."

Lorne shook her head. "I didn't really mean that. You see, Pete died in my arms... That's what I never want to happen again. His death still haunts me, but it's also what drives me on. You see, he was like a brother to me. Pete didn't have any family, and I kind of took him under my wing. He was Charlie's godfather, too." She inhaled deeply and put a forkful of rice in her mouth.

"Oh crap! I'm so sorry. All I'd heard was that he'd been killed in the line of duty."

Lorne gave a brief nod. "Come on. That's enough maudlin chat for one evening."

They finished their meal, rinsed their plates, and took their wine through to the lounge. Out of habit, Lorne put the TV onto the BBC news but dimmed the sound down low. Then she asked Katy about her experience in the force and her meteoric rise up the ranks.

At first, Katy appeared to be reluctant to divulge much of her private life. Then she settled back in the sofa, tucked her legs under her backside, and said, "It's nothing to write home about, really. I joined the force at eighteen. I'm kind of like you, in that I struggled in a male-dominated world to gain recognition. Then one day, I stumbled across a bit of information that broke a case wide open, one of the big cases the team was working on. My DCI had been on this gang's tail for a few years." She clicked her fingers together then continued, "All of a sudden, I was the best cop on his team, and he put my name forward to take the sergeant's exam."

Lorne sipped her wine, and her brow furrowed. "Oh, right. So your promotion had nothing to do with the fact that your parents know Superintendent Greenfall, then?"

Katy seemed surprised by her question and shifted position on the sofa a few times before she responded, "Is that what you've heard?"

Lorne felt awkward under her scrutinising glare. Gone was the relaxed manner Katy had shown since they had arrived home. *Damn, what did you say that for?* "I thought I heard something like that on the grapevine. Never mind. I probably misheard," she quickly back-pedalled. But she could tell the damage had already been done. "What do your parents do?"

"Mum's an accountant, and Dad's retired, although he still participates as a JP."

A Justice of the Peace, eh? Maybe that's how Greenfall knows him. "What did he do before he retired?" Lorne asked, intrigued.

"Dad was a property lawyer in Manchester. He retired a few years back. Wish I could retire at fifty-five," Katy stated, appearing to look a little more relaxed again.

Lorne's thoughts drifted, thinking about how nice it would be to retire early. Then out of the corner of her eye, an image on the TV screen caught her attention. Diving for the control, she turned up the volume. "Sorry…"

The picture was of a reporter in the mountains of Afghanistan and the breaking news banner read: *British Agent caught by the Taliban.*

Chapter Sixteen

Lorne picked up the portable phone and ran into the kitchen under Katy's amazed gaze. "Dad? Have you seen the news?" she asked, pacing the kitchen, and running a frantic hand through her hair.

"Lorne, whatever is the matter, child?"

"It's Tony—"

"What? Lorne, take a deep breath and tell me what's happened."

Lorne sucked in a few breaths and let them out, then tried again. "The news, Dad. A reporter in Afghanistan is saying there are reports that a British agent has been captured."

She heard a chair being scraped on the other end and her father flopping into it.

"Now, Lorne, you know half their stories are conjecture. If it's breaking news I doubt all the facts are right."

"But, Dad, they wouldn't report it if there wasn't at least a glimmer of truth in it, surely?"

Her father remained silent for a few seconds, contemplating her words. "Okay, here's what I would do. Wait until you hear something official from HQ before you start believing the reports. Have you heard from Tony?"

"No. That's why I'm so concerned. He *always* rings me. Without fail. I know something has happened to him, I can feel it." Her hand clutched her stomach as if he was in the room with her as tears slipped from her eyes.

"I know, love. My advice would be to keep strong until HQ get in touch. Do you want me to come over and sit with you?"

"No, I have a visitor."

"Oh, who?"

"Katy, my new partner. She, umm… Well, she's going to be staying with me for a few days."

"As you wish, love. I'm sure Tony will be in touch soon. He's probably just out of communication range. Try not to worry too much. Get some rest, and I'll ring you tomorrow."

"I'll try, Dad. Thanks. I'll call you if I hear anything. Good night."

She hung up and put the kettle on. Katy joined her in the kitchen a few seconds later. "Sorry, Lorne. I didn't mean to eavesdrop. Is there anything I can do?"

"I need you to keep quiet about this, Katy. Tony's on a secret mission. Whatever you heard, scrub it from your memory now. I'm sure he'll be okay."

Katy eyed her with pity, which didn't sit well with Lorne. "If you need to talk, I'm here."

Trying to show that she was coping with the situation, she smiled. "Hey, we're a right pair, aren't we? I invited you here to ease your discomfort, and now you've walked into this."

Katy shrugged. "That's life, I suppose. There's always something out there to throw us off-balance."

"How about a treat?" Lorne asked, determined not to dwell on something that was out of her control.

"What do you mean? In my house, a take-away is a treat." Katy smiled and raised a questioning eyebrow.

"Ah, in this household, a take-away means it's pig out night and is generally followed by a tub of ice cream."

Katy's eyes almost popped out of her head. "A whole tub?"

Lorne went over to the freezer compartment of her fridge, which was situated by the back door, and pulled out two mini tubs of Häagen Dazs ice cream. The relief on Katy's face was laughable. "Name your poison: sticky toffee pudding or chocolate and cream."

Katy puffed out her cheeks. "I'm not sure I can." Her usually flat stomach protruded, and she patted it with both hands. "I'm so full."

"Go on. Be a devil. It'll do us both the world of good to indulge. Just this once, I promise. Then we'll have a salad tomorrow to make up for our naughtiness."

Sighing, Katy nodded. "If that's an order, I better comply."

"That's my girl. Now, which one?"

Katy shrugged. "I don't mind. Either."

Lorne placed the tubs behind her back. "Left or right?"

"Right," Katy said, and Lorne handed her the sticky toffee pudding option.

After a further couple of hours of general chitchat and half-watching the crap on TV, they went to bed early, at around ten. They left for work about eight thirty the next morning. Katy told Lorne she looked rough, which wasn't exactly music to her ears, and insisted she should drive to work.

Lorne had suffered one of the worst night's sleep she'd ever had to endure. Every time she closed her eyes, she saw an image of Tony tied up in a cave with a guard standing over him. Yes, she was blessed with an overactive imagination, but that was due to Tony filling her in on a few cases he and his colleagues had been involved in over the couple of years she'd known him. His harrowing words were now haunting her every waking moment and rattling around in her head.

Lorne had just settled down to open her post when the phone rang on her desk. She placed the phone between her cheek and her shoulder. "DI Simpkins. How can I help?"

"Lorne, it's Patti."

She dropped the letter she was inspecting on the desk and gave Patti, the pathologist, her full attention. "Oh, hi. I was going to either call you or come and see you today."

"You were? We'll I've just saved you a job. Just ringing up to see if you received the post reports on the kids?"

"I did, thanks. Shame they didn't show up anything. It was worth a shot."

"Is everything all right? You don't sound your chirpy self. I know we haven't dealt with each other much, but I can usually tell what someone's like within a few minutes of meeting them."

"Funny, I've got a dog like that."

"Sorry?" Patti asked, puzzled.

"Oh nothing. It's just a personal issue I have to deal with. Thanks for your concern, Patti."

"If ever you want to chat, you know where I am. Maybe we could have lunch one day?"

"Maybe when Tony gets back."

"Sorry?" Patti asked, confusion in her tone. "I take it Tony is your other half. Is he away at the moment?"

Because of Patti's gentle manner, Lorne felt she could trust the new pathologist, and before she could engage her brain, she had told the woman about the news report.

"Bloody hell! I'm not saying that about the situation, I just didn't realise we had that much in common."

"Really? In what way?" Lorne asked, reclining back in her chair.

"My husband is in the forces. Special forces, actually, and he's out in Afghanistan on a mission at this moment, too."

"Wow! Have you heard from him lately? How long has he been out there?"

"Between you and me, he's been out there a couple of months. They're after some kind of drug warlord. I haven't heard from him in over two weeks, but that's nothing unusual, Lorne. Communications are down most of the time over there. They think the Taliban regularly jam the communications equipment. When he does call, it only lasts for a few minutes, if that."

At last, information that would help settle her stomach and stop her mind thinking the unthinkable. Despite feeling like crap, Lorne smiled. "Thanks, Patti. Talking to you has really helped me put things into perspective. Damn reporters! I'll get back to you soon, and we'll make arrangements to have lunch or a celebratory dinner when the guys return."

"Glad to be of some assistance. Try not to worry, and keep your chin up. Speak soon."

Lorne replaced the phone and breathed out a relieved sigh, then gave herself a good talking to. "Right, now you're not to worry about things that you have no control over. Until you hear something definite about Tony's status, you're going to give your all to this case." A soft knock on the door interrupted her. "Come in."

Katy pushed the door open and placed two cups of vending machine coffee on the desk and sat down. "Sorry, I thought you were on the phone, didn't want to interrupt."

Lorne felt her cheeks redden, and her gaze drifted out the window to the tower block offices beyond. "I've just given myself a good talking to." She picked up her coffee and took a sip of the rich roasted blend before her eyes met Katy's. "Between us, we're a fine pair at the moment, aren't we?"

Katy's gaze rose to the ceiling. "How about we listen to your advice and concentrate on the case?" She stood up, left the office, and returned seconds later, holding the files they'd picked up at the security firm. She handed one to Lorne.

They studied the files in silence for a few minutes, until Lorne looked up and asked, "What date did the Dobbses have their security fitted?"

"April fifteenth."

"Hmm… The Kelly's had their system fitted a week earlier, on the eighth."

"That sounds like another one of those coincidences we keep hearing about," Katy said, still reading through the file.

"Well, that's all I can find in here." Lorne looked at her watch and saw it had just turned ten thirty. "I'll just try and get on top of the post, and then we'll head over to the pub, see if we can track down this Zac fella. Can you see what evidence the team has managed to collect so far?"

Katy took her drink with her and left the office. Lorne rifled through the post like a woman possessed and had everything neatly stacked in the relevant trays on her desk within forty-five minutes.

* * *

They pulled up outside The Cross Keys, on the other side of the city, around an hour and a half later. The pub matched the area, run down and in desperate need of rejuvenation. As Underhill had stated, a huge-breasted blonde barmaid was anchored behind the bar. When she opened her mouth, the decibels would've sent a sound level monitor shooting off the scale.

As they walked up to the grimy, chipped wooden bar, one of the punters sitting at the bar leaned over and tried to grope one of the barmaid's prized assets. She slapped his hand away and laughed, a laugh that would rival any wild hyena's.

Lorne and Katy looked at each and shook their heads in disgust. Eyeing the clientele, Lorne reached into her pocket to check that her pepper spray was handy. It was clear they'd need to be vigilant in this intimidating environment.

"Two orange juices, please," Lorne said, without the hint of a smile.

The blonde, whose roots were showing, eyed her with disdain and took two bottles of juice from the shelf, along with two glasses, and slammed them down on the bar in front of the two detectives.

"Five quid," the woman spat out.

Lorne knew the price had been inflated for their benefit by the way the two guys at the bar were sniggering.

After Lorne paid the barmaid, they picked up their drinks and headed for the back of the rundown, smoke-stained pub. They could feel three sets of eyes following them to the torn vinyl bench. Once seated, they had a great view of who was coming in and going out.

Ordinarily their surveillance would have been carried out discreetly outside, but Lorne had decided to see what the inside of the pub held. The problem was that two women dressed in smart overcoats screamed 'police' and alerted the other punters.

"Friendly bunch, aren't they?" Lorne said, wiping the lipstick stain off the rim of her glass with a tissue.

"I've come across more friendliness on a drive through Longleat," Katy said drolly out of the corner of her mouth.

"I can't see anyone matching Zac's description yet. I suppose it's still early."

They nattered away for the next twenty minutes or so until a slim-built man in his mid–late twenties stormed into the pub.

The two men at the bar and the barmaid looked up. Their smiles simultaneously slipped from their faces the second they saw who the customer was.

Lorne elbowed Katy gently in the ribs. "Heads up! Ginger alert."

The man had obviously already had a few drinks too many. He swaggered up to the bar and placed a foot on the rail at the bottom, almost toppling over in the process. "Got any news for me?"

The blonde raised an eyebrow and her lip turned up. "I told you yesterday. I don't know nothin'."

"And I told you I thought you were lying to me. Now give us a name, or—"

"Or what?" A voice bellowed from the doorway. A man in a black, heavy wool overcoat was standing there, two bouncer-type goons on either side of him.

"You?" The redhead, who they suspected was Zac, spun round fast and lost his footing. He slammed into the stool next to him with a grunt.

Out of the corner of her eye, Lorne spotted the barmaid clear her throat and point in their direction with her head. Immediately the guy and his heavies looked over at them with hatred in their eyes.

Lorne picked up her glass, averted her eyes, and murmured, "We've been made. Don't look at him. Just keep talking."

Their avoidance tactic appeared to work, if only for a short time, as the man in the overcoat turned his attention back to the redhead. "I hear you been asking about me, squirt." He and the two goons took a few steps forward until they were a few feet in front of the other man.

"You?" Zac repeated.

The man in the overcoat glanced in Lorne's direction again. Leaning forward, he whispered in Zac's face.

Lorne was fuming that she couldn't hear what was being said, but Zac's reaction spoke volumes.

He took a swing at the man in the overcoat, missing his target and ending up on his backside on the floor. "I'll get you for that," he slurred and attempted to stand up, only to flop back down, exhausted.

The three newcomers and the punters sitting at the bar all laughed, which made Zac kick out and try to get to his feet, only to fail again.

Lorne watched the somewhat comical goings-on with interest, making mental notes of each of the characters involved. The pub wasn't on her patch, so she had no idea who the criminals were. It would mean spending hours trawling through the database when she got back, unless she could find out their names. She doubted anyone in the pub would be willing to volunteer any names. Discreetly, she placed her phone on the table in front of her and angled it in the men's direction. She hit the button repeatedly hoping she had managed to capture a few good images. Only time would tell on that one.

Katy smiled at her and did well to keep the trivial conversation going between them that served as a distraction to anyone looking their way.

Eventually, Zac stood up and staggered towards the man in the overcoat, only for the man's two henchmen to stand in his way. Zac pointed at the man. "You ain't heard the last of this."

The man shrugged. "Neither have you and yours, boy. Take that warning back with ya."

The thugs shoved him and sent him reeling to the floor, before all three of them, after a quick warning glance in the detectives' direction, left the pub.

After another couple of minutes, Lorne and Katy finished their drinks and moved toward the pub's entrance. Before they got there, Zac approached Lorne and stood in front of her. His eyes screwed up in distaste. "What ya doin' here, filth?"

Put off by the odour of stale booze on his breath rather than his threatening behaviour, Lorne stepped into his personal space and beckoned him so she could whisper in his ear. "In case you hadn't noticed, Zac, it's a free country. We can go where we like. Oh, and for your information, your little performance has just put you on our radar."

He pulled his head back. His eyes were glassy and drooping because of the drink he'd consumed. "What d'ya mean? What radar?"

Lorne tapped the side of her nose and motioned to Katy that they were leaving. Zac shouted after her, "You old tart, what d'ya mean?"

They heard the punters at the bar and the barmaid shouting and telling Zac to 'Give it a rest and go home.'

Chapter Seventeen

When they arrived at Styles Interiors, their unannounced visit seemed to rattle the owner of the business, and Lorne couldn't help wondering why.

Danielle Styles was a sleek-looking, black-haired woman in her early–mid thirties, stylishly dressed in a beige boucle suit that had large, prominent gold buttons embedded with the Chanel emblem. Their surroundings echoed the opulence Lorne had witnessed at the two murder scenes she'd recently attended.

Towards the rear of the expansive showroom was row upon row of exquisite large rolls of fabric, arranged by colour, with the paler colours at the top and the darker ones at the bottom. To the left stood dozens of mirrors along one wall, mostly ornate with gold frames, but Lorne spotted a few with modern touches too. The rest of the showroom was sectioned off into lounge, dining room, and bedroom areas. Not a shabby-looking sofa or chipped table in sight.

Digging her warrant card out of her coat pocket, Lorne flashed it at the woman, who was obviously fighting to keep her composure.

"Ms. Styles? I'm DI Simpkins, and this is DS Foster. Is there somewhere private where we can have a little chat?"

The woman examined the gold watch loosely draped across her tiny wrist and sighed. "I can spare you five minutes before an important client comes in."

If the woman thought her schedule would put Lorne off, she had another think coming. "Let's put it this way, Ms. Styles: either you find the time to see me here, or we can ask our questions in a cold, damp interview room back at the station. I know which I'd prefer."

Styles spun on her heel, her hair and skirt flicking out in the spin, and walked swiftly through the showroom. Katy and Lorne fell into step behind her. The woman's office was comprised of a wall of glass that looked out onto the showroom they'd just left. Styles swept behind her large smoked-top table and daintily sat in a leather office chair while Lorne and Katy rejected her offer to sit on the three-seater sofa, and chose to stand.

The woman stretched her long slim neck up to look at Lorne and asked, "So, what's this all about, Inspector?"

"We're just making enquiries at this stage, Ms. Styles. I presume you know that a couple of your clients have been burgled in the last few days?"

Nodding, Styles replied, "Yes, it's a dreadful situation."

And how would she know that if the news hasn't broken on TV yet? In the same level voice, Lorne asked, "Can you tell me how you got the contracts for the Dobbses and the Kellys?"

The woman's perfectly preened eyebrows met as she frowned. "I'm not with you?"

"You seem an intelligent enough woman to me. I really can't ask my question any more simply, Ms. Styles."

The woman broke eye contact with Lorne, sat back in her chair, and placed her elbows on the chair's thickly padded arms. "Most of my work comes from word of mouth. People recommend me all the time."

"Ah, I see. So you did some work for the Dobbses, and the Kellys went on to employ you, is that right?"

"I can't remember which way round it was, but…" She stood up and walked over to the cabinet and pulled up the concertinaed front, returning with a moss-green-coloured file, which she placed open on the desk. "Ah, here we are… Yes, the Kellys had their makeover completed before the Dobbses."

"And where did the Kellys' recommendation come from?" Lorne asked, a niggling feeling beginning in the depths of her stomach.

The woman rifled through the papers, going back and forth to several sheets before she cleared her throat and told them, "Umm… I believe the recommendation came from a friend of mine, Kim."

Katy took out her notebook. "Do you have a surname for her?"

"Smalling. We go back years. What does this have to do with your case, Inspector?"

"We're just in the process of joining up the dots, Ms. Styles. I wonder if you would mind giving us a copy of your client list?"

The woman gathered the sheets together and stuffed them back in the folder, then held it protectively close to her chest. "Don't you need some kind of warrant or court order or something?"

Here we go again. "Only if you have something to hide. *Do* you have something to hide?" Lorne approached the desk, flattened her palms on it and leaned over.

The woman blinked her thickly mascaraed eyelashes quite a few times before she answered, "Me? What would I have to hide?"

"I don't know. We'll wait while you copy the documents." Lorne's smile pulled her lips into a straight line across her teeth.

Styles leapt to her feet and took the file to an outer office. Lorne expected the woman to rejoin them and to leave the menial task of copying to an office secretary or someone. When she didn't, Lorne surmised her actions meant that she intended to avoid them. Styles returned with a pile of papers around ten minutes later.

Lorne accepted the pile of papers and gave them to Katy. She held out her hand for Styles to shake, another trick her father had taught her at the beginning of her career: You can tell a lot from a person's character in the way they shake your hand.

The thing that struck Lorne most about their handshake was how sweaty and clammy Styles' palm was. She recollected her father's words: 'A sweaty palm is a sure sign that person is guilty of something or has something to hide.' She left the office and wandered back to the car, wondering which category Styles fit into.

* * *

It was getting on for five o'clock by the time they tackled the city traffic and arrived back at the station.

John was anxiously pacing up and down just inside the door to the incident room. "Ah, there you are, ma'am. The DCI would like a word."

"Everything all right, John? Did he give you a clue what about?"

He shook his head vigorously and rubbed his hands together anxiously. "No, ma'am."

"What aren't you telling me, John?"

"Nothing, ma'am."

Lorne knew by the way he was fidgeting that something was up. She turned to Katy. "You make a start on those. I'll see what the boss wants, and then we'll head home for the night."

The DCI's personal assistant leapt out of her seat and knocked on his door the second she saw Lorne, heightening her stress levels further. The wily fox didn't do things like that without reason.

"DI Simpkins is here, sir." The assistant held the door open, and Lorne walked past her.

"Get us some coffee, will you?" DCI Roberts said.

"Not for me, thanks. Sir?"

He motioned for her to take a seat, and with her eyes locked on his, she lowered herself gently into the chair. She heard him exhale a deep breath as he sat down opposite her.

"I had a call this afternoon," he said almost reluctantly.

Lorne settled back into her chair and crossed one leg over the other. "Okay, enough of the dramatics, Sean. From whom?"

What he said next knocked the wind out of her and left her clutching her chest and gasping for breath.

Chapter Eighteen

"Oh, my God! Sean, tell me it's not true," she said, tears misting her eyes and seeping onto her colourless cheeks.

"I wish I could, Lorne. But MI6 have confirmed it. They wanted to tell you themselves, but I said it would be better coming from a friend. What can I do to help?"

Stunned, Lorne simply stared at him and lifted her shoulders slightly. "You can tell me that I'll see him again. That I'll hold him in my arms again."

"It breaks my heart to say this, but we both know I can't guarantee that. The Taliban have a habit of playing by their own rules. You need to prepare yourself for every eventuality," he said gravely.

Her eyes met his, and she shook her head vehemently. "I refuse to give up on him. I know his love for me will get him through this. It has to."

"I didn't mean to sound heartless, Lorne, but—"

"I know you didn't. But if I give up on him now, then I might as well give up breathing, Sean. He's my soul mate. The air that I breathe—" She broke off as a hard lump lodged in her throat.

"I'm so sorry, Lorne. After all the shit you've had to contend with over the years, Tony was the bright spark—"

"Is! Is, not *was*. He's still alive, and while there's a tiny hope left, I'm sure he'll return home to me. Do you mind if I ring Dad?"

"No, of course not. Do it from here. I'll give you some peace." He rose from his chair and walked round his desk. He squeezed her shoulder gently as he passed.

"Dad, thank God you're home."

"Lorne? Whatever is the matter, child?"

"The reports were true, Dad."

Her father groaned, and she heard him kick a chair or something. "Damn! Have HQ confirmed that?"

"Yes, Dad. Sean's just told me. What am I going to do?" she sobbed fresh tears.

"Are you up to telling me what happened, love?" he asked tentatively.

"Apparently the Taliban captured him up in the mountains. He was hiding out in a cave near the drug warlord he was after. They've publicly flogged and tortured him. Oh, Dad…"

"I know, love. For his sake and yours, please remain positive. You hear it all the time on TV about rescue attempts. Tony's one of MI6's greatest assets. They won't give up on him, and neither should we."

It was just the kind of hopeful words she wanted to hear. Her father always managed to say the right thing, to keep her buoyant when all those around her thought the worst of a given situation. His time on the force had taught him that positivity overwhelmed any likely negativity in instances such as this.

"But they've already killed another agent. What's to stop them from killing Tony?"

"That's a logical question, sweetheart. But look at it this way. They killed the other agent, and Tony was sent out. The Taliban know that MI6 will keep sending agents to replace those killed. They'll probably be rethinking their plans as we speak. If not… and I'm going to be cruel here. If they're not about to change their strategy, they would've already killed him by now. Instead they've only flogged and tortured him. I say *only*… but you know what I mean."

Lorne blew out a relieved breath when she realised her father had a point. Fresh hope surrounded her heart and a slight smile touched her lips. "Thanks, Dad."

"No problem, love. I know you've got company with that lassie staying with you, but if you'd like me to come and stay for a few days, I will."

"I'll be all right, Dad. You have my word that I will stay strong until all possible hope has diminished." It was the exact same words her father had said when her mother was lying in the hospital dying of cancer.

They both said they loved each other and then hung up.

Seconds later, Sean entered the room behind her. "Everything all right?"

"I know you were listening, Sean. No point in denying it."

"Ah! I forgot you were a shit hot detective." He chuckled and perched his backside on the edge of the desk in front of her. "Seriously, if you need a chat, my door is always open."

Lorne nodded, and their eyes met. "I know and I'm grateful."

"If you want some time off, I'll understand and back you all the way."

One of her eyebrows rose up quizzically. "Did I have time off when Baldwin kidnapped Charlie?"

"No, you didn't. But this is different, Lorne," he stated, patting her hand with his.

"I can't sit at home all day wondering... I'd rather be here throwing myself into the job, surrounded by friends."

"I understand, totally. If I were in your shoes, I'd feel the same way. If the need arises to come and vent or to kick something or someone, don't be afraid to knock on my door."

She stood up and moved to the door before she responded. "Thanks. I appreciate it. Katy and I are going to call it a day now, if that's okay?"

"Of course. Fill me in on the case tomorrow, okay?"

"Sorry, we went to—"

He raised a hand to stop her. "Unless you've uncovered some case-breaking evidence, it can wait until tomorrow. Go home and *try* to get some rest. You've got my home number if you need me, all right?"

"Thanks, sir. I'll be here bright and early to run through the case with you, then."

"That's a date, Inspector. Now, shoo!"

When she walked through the outer office, even the wily fox had a sympathetic expression. Any other time, Lorne would've bitten the woman's head off. In this instance, she decided the woman's heart was in the right place and gave her a brief nod of acceptance.

Katy insisted she should drive home while Lorne filled her in on what had happened to Tony, with the understanding that it went no further.

All the way through her horrific tale, Katy shook her head and gasped several times. After unburdening herself, Lorne spent the rest of the journey in dazed silence. And when Henry came to meet her at the door, she bent down to hug him and broke down.

"Oh, Henry, what am I going to do without him?"

The dog whimpered. Katy squeezed past her, patted Lorne on the shoulder, and ruffled the dog's head. Then she went through to the kitchen and opened the back door for the collie, to be ready for when his mistress released him.

Sensing her need was greater than his, Henry sat and licked the salty streaks on her cheeks.

Several fraught minutes later, she kissed him and sent him on his way. Lorne followed him into the kitchen where Katy was pouring boiling water into two cups. "I'm sorry."

"For what? Being human and having normal feelings? Everyone has their breaking point. My old Nan used to say, 'A good cry set the world to rights.' You need to get it out of your system before you can begin to see things more clearly."

Lorne smiled, took the offered cup of coffee, and moved to the back door. "When did you become so sensible?"

"I've always been quite an expert on human nature. I just find it a struggle to take onboard my old Nan's advice. I can dish it out, but as far as heeding it goes... Nah, it isn't going to happen."

Lorne dried the dog's paws on the towel hanging on the rail by the back door and looked up at Katy. "I'll feed Henry, but would you mind fending for yourself tonight? There are plenty of ready meals in the freezer compartment, and the microwave is easy-to-use."

Katy's head tilted questioningly.

"I'm not hungry. I thought I'd have a soak in the bath and grab an early night," Lorne clarified.

Her partner nodded. "Sure. But my old Nan used to say—"

Lorne smiled and interrupted her, "Yeah, I know, something like 'Never skip a meal in a crisis.'"

"Something like that. Give me a shout later if you want me to make you a sandwich or something. There's a David Attenborough documentary on that I wanted to see anyway, so don't worry about me."

Lorne gave Henry his evening meal, then disappeared upstairs, still surprised by Katy's comment that she was interested in Attenborough's work. *Not a thing you'd consider a youngster entertaining nowadays. Or someone of Lorne's age, come to that.*

The half-hour soak in her wonderfully fragrant lavender foam bath helped ease the tension in her body and put things into perspective a little. But she entered the bedroom and saw the picture Charlie had taken of Tony and herself down by the river. They were the epitome of happiness, laughing and looking adoringly at each other. Her newfound resolve teetered on the edge of the precipice.

To take her mind off things, she picked up her Kindle and started reading the paranormal mystery by Linda Prather that she'd downloaded the week before, after Charlie had raved about how good it was.

She drifted off to sleep a little while later, but she woke up every few hours crying out Tony's name.

Chapter Nineteen

The next morning, her stomach was complaining so much that she got up at six thirty and fixed herself a fry-up.

Katy appeared sometime after seven thirty and helped herself to a bowl of cereal. "What's on the agenda today?"

Lorne appreciated the fact that her partner hadn't referred to how rough she looked. Maybe the light touch of makeup she'd applied had successfully masked her pallor.

"First of all, I need to bring Roberts up-to-date on the case, not that we have much to go on. While I'm doing that, I thought you could team up with AJ, to download the pictures I took on my camera yesterday and see if you can come up with a match on the database."

"Okay. This AJ, I get the impression he's a bit of a ladies' man. Is he?"

She laughed. "We used to say he likes his cars fast and his women even faster! I'm not sure if things have changed or not while I've been away. One thing, though…"

"Oh, what's that?"

"You two have something in common."

Katy screwed up her cute nose and asked, "What's that?"

"You come from wealthy families."

"I didn't say my family is wealthy," Katy responded defensively.

"Oh didn't you? My mistake. AJ's father is a lord. I'm not saying he can't be trusted, but we tend to tread carefully around him. Wouldn't want to upset him, if you know what I mean." She tapped her nose.

"Crikey! What's he working in the police for?"

"He was told to get out and fend for himself. He's good at his job, though. Conscientious and reliable—just your average team member, but be careful all the same."

"Message received."

* * *

"What the hell happened to you last night?"

Zac sat at the kitchen table, holding his sore head in his hands, groaning as his brother's voice reverberated through the low-ceilinged kitchen and slapped him round the face.

"You wouldn't believe me if I told you."

"Try me," his brother retorted impatiently.

"I got bladdered and picked up a bird."

"All right, spare me the gory details, will you? What happened down the pub?"

Zac gulped noisily and lifted his head up to look at his brother. "Shit happened."

Drumming his fingers on the countertop of the island, his brother asked, "What's that supposed to mean? What the fuck are you on about?"

"I was just going to start asking around... You know, like you asked me to. When Denman walked in with his heavies."

"And?" His brother came towards him, wearing a menacing expression, and sat in the chair next to him.

"He told me to... to pass on a message... to you," Zac stammered, sensing his brother would blow his top any minute.

"Get on with it, for fuck's sake."

"He said, 'We know what you and yours are up to, and it's game on,'" Zac told him before taking a sip of his coffee.

"I should've guessed he'd be behind it. He'll be after payback."

"Yeah, that's what I thought. What we gonna do about it?"

"*You're* gonna go see that Underhill and see what he knows. Beat it out of him if you have to."

Grimacing, Zac moaned. "What, today? Couldn't I leave it till tomorrow?" The look on his brother's face told him he had asked the stupidest of questions. Again.

* * *

Lorne left Katy and AJ downloading the photos and went to Roberts' office.

"No need to ask if you slept all right last night," he said, pointing at the chair.

She shrugged. "I think you'd be the same, given the circumstances. Wouldn't you?"

"I have no doubt about that, Inspector. That's why I told you to take a few days off."

"I'd rather be here, if it's all the same. About the case, sir…"

"Go on," Roberts said.

"DS Foster and I had quite an eventful day yesterday. The guy at 'Trust Us'—yeah, I know—when we questioned him about being connected to the footballers and obtaining their contracts, he mentioned that he'd met a Zac at a pub."

"As you do," Roberts said, tutting.

"Anyway, we went down there to try and find out who this bloke is, when who should stroll in but this Zac. Drunk as a skunk, shouting the odds. A couple of minutes later, three other men walked in." Roberts sat forward in his chair. Lorne continued, "They got in each other's faces for a while—"

"What about?"

"I wish I knew. This Zac started off shouting at this other guy. In response, the other guy leaned forward and whispered something. I couldn't hear what was said, but judging by the way Zac reacted, I'd say he goaded him in some way."

"So what happened next?"

"The barmaid warned them that we were there, and after a few warning glances directed our way, things died down. The three men left within minutes of arriving. We waited a few minutes, then tried to leave ourselves, but this Zac stood in our way. He called us a few choice names and I had to warn him to back off. I ended up telling him he was now firmly on our radar."

Roberts chuckled. "I can just imagine the scene. So, did you recognize any of the men?"

"That's just it: the pub isn't on our patch, but I took discreet pictures of the scene on my phone. Not sure how good the pictures will be, though. What with finding out about Tony yesterday, it slipped my mind to check them when I got home."

He waved away her explanation. "That's understandable, Lorne. You'll get on to it today, right?"

"Katy and AJ are on it now. Back to yesterday, after the pub, we paid a visit to the designer who was contracted to kit out the Dobbses' and Kellys' homes. She's a sassy individual, on her guard the minute we stepped foot in her swanky showroom. I came away with the client files. I'm going to go through them today to see what turns up."

"Anything else?"

"Not yet… I hope to compare the files of the security firm and the designer. Something smells more than a little fishy there. But I get the sense that these guys are just the tip of the iceberg."

"Care to enlighten me further?" he asked, relaxing back in his chair.

"You know me and my instincts. My immediate thoughts are, looking at the two people concerned—the designer and the security firm guy—I doubt they'd have the brains or the guts to get involved. Whereas this Zac fella is a totally different story."

"Why don't you delegate comparing the files to DS Fox or someone and concentrate on finding out more about this Zac, then?"

Lorne wrinkled her nose and remained silent.

Roberts hit the desk lightly with his hand. "Dumb of me to think of that, really, knowing what a control freak you are."

Her jaw dropped open until she saw his face crack into a smile. "Okay, I'll give you that one. It does make sense. I'll put John on it and get delving into this guy's past—if I can find a name for him, that is."

She rose out of her chair and walked to the door.

"You will," he called after her confidently.

Chapter Twenty

When Lorne entered the incident room, she noticed how cosy her two sergeants appeared to be. Sitting alongside each other, both Katy and AJ were grinning broadly and nudging shoulders.

Hmm... Interesting. Maybe they have more in common than their parents, after all.

She advanced towards them and cleared her throat when she reached AJ's desk. "How's it going?" she asked, cocking an eyebrow.

The pair separated and leaned away from each other. AJ started stammering, "Er... I've downloaded the pictures, ma'am, I'm just going... I mean, we're just going through the database now."

"Were the pictures okay?"

He smiled and shook his head. "Let's just say you won't be winning any quality awards for them."

"Cheeky sod. As long as you can use some of them. Let me know what you come up with."

Katy went to stand up, but Lorne put her hand on her shoulder and gently pushed her back down. "No, carry on searching the database with AJ. The more eyes we have on this, the better. I have a feeling this will end up being a key part of the investigation. I'll be in my office, doing my bit."

"Whatever you say, ma'am."

If Lorne didn't know any better, she would have thought the look on Katy's face was one of relief. "Has anyone seen DS Fox?"

Molly answered her in a hushed voice. "He's nipped to the gents, ma'am. Anything I can do for you?"

Molly's eagerness made up Lorne's mind for her. "Actually, Molly, you'd probably be more suited for the task I had in mind, anyway. Come into my office, will you?"

In the office, Lorne picked up the relevant files and went over what she wanted Molly to do with them. Molly told her to give her the rest of the day, and that she'd hopefully have a result for her by the end of the shift, if there was anything to find.

Satisfied she'd chosen the right person for the job, Lorne grabbed a coffee from the machine and started ringing a few old contacts. About an hour into her mission, she realised with sadness but complete understanding that many of her colleagues, people she had worked well with over the years, had retired from the force.

It brought her own situation home, her doubts about returning to work and giving up her newly found and interesting career. Not forgetting the turmoil she was going through with regard to Tony being on the MIA list. What if he never returned home to her? What on earth would she do without him? She'd become dependent on his support and love, and to have it ripped away from her at this early stage in their relationship... She feared it would destroy her.

Her father's words filled her head: 'Keep strong, girl; never give up.' She nodded and took a deep breath before placing another call. "DI Holland, please."

"Directing you now, ma'am," the girl on the switchboard said.

"DI Holland. How can I help?"

"Steve, long time no hear... It's Lorne Simpkins."

"Wow, now there's a name I thought I'd never hear again. How the dickens are you?"

Lorne and Steve had been through Hendon together. During training and exams, usually she or Steve came out on top, with the other coming in close second. Their relationship had always been a friendly rivalry, and despite being in different forces, their paths had crossed several times in the past, with satisfactory results.

She was glad he sounded pleased to hear from her. "What's the old saying? 'You can't keep an old dog down.'"

They both laughed.

"Yeah. From what I've heard, many have tried over the years." He was obviously referring to the tussles she'd had with the Met's hierarchy in her last stint of serving in the force, namely with her own Superintendent Greenfall.

"Enough of the niceties. I wondered if you could help me out on a case?"

"If I can, you know I will, Lorne. Shoot."

"I'm working on a few robberies at the moment. I wouldn't usually deal with them, but the robbers decided to leave some murder victims at the scene."

"Go on," he said, sounding intrigued.

"Anyway, I was in your neck of the woods yesterday following up on a lead when I kind of stumbled on something."

"Okay, it's getting interesting now."

"I know it's a long shot, but have you come across a Zac?"

"Zac what?"

Sighing, she told him, "That's just it. That's all I have for now. I was hoping something might ring a bell with you if I gave you a description. It's sort of an unusual name," she added hopefully.

He blew out an exasperated breath before he answered. "Let's see what we can find. What description do you have?"

"Around the six foot mark, red hair, and mid–late thirties."

"Geesh, is that it?" She heard him tapping away at the keyboard and the computer making a tinging sound as though he'd punched in the wrong keys.

"That's all I've got, I'm afraid. Oh, hang on, he had a cockney accent."

"Bloody hell. You don't expect much, do you? Let me have a quick look around while you're on the phone."

"Thanks. I've got my team working on it, too, but I thought something might jolt a memory. Talking of which, when we were in the pub, another three tough guys came in."

"And?"

"There was a bit of a contretemps among them. I couldn't hear what was said, but the way Zac reacted, I'd hazard a guess that he'd been warned off."

"That's more like it. Give me a minute or two."

A knock sounded on her office door, she placed her hand over the mouthpiece. "Come in." AJ stuck his head round the door. The sergeant looked pleased with himself. "What have you got?"

"I've managed to match a few of your dubious photos, ma'am. I've come up with the name Zac Murray."

Lorne held up a finger telling AJ to wait and repeated the name into the phone and heard Holland bang his fist on the desk.

"Of course. Zac Murray. He's been a bit quiet lately. I must say I'm surprised he's involved in any murders, though. I've always had him down as a petty criminal. He used to go around with a Carl somebody. Let's see if I can locate him."

While Holland tapped away at his computer again, Lorne asked AJ, "Did you manage to find any names for the other guys?"

Disappointed, he screwed his nose up and shook his head. "Sorry, ma'am."

"It doesn't matter. AJ, let's see what DI Holland comes up with. Why don't you and Katy grab some lunch?" AJ's brow knitted together. "I mean, break for something to eat, and we'll continue after lunch. I've got a few calls to make."

"Can I get you a sandwich or something, ma'am?" AJ asked.

"If you're going to the canteen, I'll have a tuna and mayo, please." She smiled, and he left the office, closing the door behind him.

She had a feeling she would need to have a word in both AJ's and Katy's ears before long. Although she was pleased they appeared to be getting on so well, relationships between team members didn't go down too well with either her or the force. Plus there was Katy's boyfriend to consider. To stir up that particular hornet's nest would involve yet more trouble for Katy. She made a mental note to have a proper chat with Katy when they got home, maybe while the young sergeant was packing her bag for her weekend trip to see her parents up north.

"Here we go: Carl Ward. Both been in the nick for a few months. Like I say, petty criminals; shoplifting, mainly. Caught nicking booze from an off-licence once or twice. Nothing you'd count as major."

"Maybe they picked up a few tips while they were banged up," Lorne said.

"You're probably right there. That's usually the case. Maybe they've joined up with someone else. Zac's the type who has trouble knowing what time of day it is. Someone needs to pull his strings."

"Interesting. Okay, Steve. Thanks for all your help. If you think of anything else or another name crops up, can you let me know?"

"Sure. I'll be in touch. I'll ask around, see what I can find out about the other guys for you."

"Cheers. You're a star." She hung up and was surprised when the phone rang again. "DI Simpkins."

"Lorne, oh God. I'm so sorry, hon."

Her sister's concerned voice brought unwelcome tears to her eyes. Damn. She had been holding it together so well, too.

"Hi, Jade. Did Dad ring you?"

"Of course he did, although I would've rather heard the news from you. How are you holding up?"

"Sorry, love, I didn't want to worry you. I'm trying to keep myself occupied so I don't imagine all sorts of things."

"What can I do to help, anything?"

Lorne could tell her sister was struggling to hold it together. Jade thought the world of Tony and had welcomed him with open arms as part of her extended family despite her fondness for Tom, whom she had known for years.

"There's not a lot any of us can do at the moment, hon, except sit and wait for news."

"Thank God you have your work to keep your mind off things."

Lorne almost laughed as she thought of the number of times Jade had chastised her for putting work before everything else—her family, her friends, even her marriage to Tom. It seemed ironic that her sister was now pleased that her work would be a distraction while she waited for news.

"Yeah, I'll vouch for that. Let's get off the subject, shall we? How are my little nephews doing?"

Cheerfully Jade replied, "Still tying me up in knots. One is keeping me awake all night because he's teething and the other is caught up in the terrible twos syndrome."

"Now you can understand why I only had the one child."

"Er... yeah. I'm totally understanding that. Although I have to tell you, at the time I thought you were nuts for not giving Charlie any siblings. Maybe if she'd had a brother or sister, she wouldn't have gone off the rails the way she did a few years back."

"I doubt it, but thanks for that insight," she replied, glancing up at the ceiling.

"I wasn't having a go, Lorne, honest."

Lorne bit down hard on her tongue and waited a few seconds before she responded. "Yeah, I know. You always manage to have some kind of dig, though, Jade, don't you?"

"Crap. I'm sorry. I don't mean to. Forget I said anything. Are you seeing Charlie at the weekend?"

It was difficult to just brush away the criticism her sister had just aired, but to keep the peace, she did. "Yep, she's coming over tonight, and we're going ice-skating over the weekend. Should be fun. Not sure what my balance will be like after all this time, though."

"You'll be fine. You were always great when we were kids. I kind of lost interest when I broke my wrist on that school trip to Bristol."

"Oh God, don't remind me. I hope you haven't tempted fate there."

They both laughed.

"They say it's like riding a bike. Once you put your skates on, there'll be no stopping you. Give me a ring in the week. Let me know how you got on or if you hear anything about Tony."

"Will do. Thanks for ringing, Jade. Give the kids a slobbery kiss for me."

They both hung up.

While Lorne ate her sandwich, she mulled over the two names that had come to light. She made plans to get her team delving deeper into each person's past during the afternoon—where they hung out, where they lived, where they were banged up, and what friendships they'd struck up inside.

Chapter Twenty-One

The pain was borderline excruciating. He eased open his swollen eye and glanced down at the blood seeping through his white linen trousers belonging to his cover as an Afghan herdsman.

It had been hours since they'd beaten him publicly for the second time. That time, the attack had been far more brutal, and the injuries he'd sustained had been far worse. Struggling to sit upright against the cave's jagged damp wall, he tore a strip of fabric from his tunic and wrapped it around the wound on his upper thigh, wincing as he pulled it tight.

The cave was compact, with barely enough room to stand up. It had a prison door at its opening, and in the darkness, Tony could just make out the skeletal remains of its former inhabitant.

Well, that doesn't bode well.

He listened for any possible movement outside but heard none. The men came twice a day with a bowl of water and a lump of bread that looked as if they'd played football with it for at least half an hour. Most of the time, they spilt three quarters of the contents of the bowl of water before they handed it to him. His lips were cracked open to the point of bleeding.

But he was alive. If they'd wanted to kill him, they would've succeeded by now. He looked down and gingerly touched his chest. Touching the whip lashings made him flinch. Instead of whipping his back, the men—three of them—took turns whipping his chest while he had been tied to a post. They had driven him, blindfolded, to a nearby town to mete out his punishment. He suspected his public beating had the intention of keeping the locals in line, more than anything. It was how the Taliban ruled, through fear.

Several other people, men and women, had been punished or tortured that day. A thief had his hands severed at the wrists. A woman, not more than twenty, who Tony presumed had been accused of adultery, had been stripped and raped by half a dozen bearded men before they had stoned her to death. The town's inhabitants had been gathered and forced to watch, with armed guards milling around behind them. Those who hid their eyes were beaten black and blue with the butts of AK-47s.

Tony had come off light so far, compared to the others; he realised that. He had no idea what the future held for him and constantly prayed for Headquarters to send reinforcements, but he feared they wouldn't, especially after already losing Simon on the mission. The thing that kept him sane was the thought of his beautiful Lorne and their forthcoming wedding. The image of her wonderful smile and the way her eyes shone when she looked at him was the one thing that kept him from giving up.

A smile spread his cracked lips as he thought of Lorne and Charlie spending time together at the ice-skating rink. Boy, he wished he was there with them now, enjoying life instead of fearing that it would come to an abrupt end at any moment.

He hadn't heard the men approach until the key clunked against the lock and the door opened. Tony pretended to be asleep. He was too weak to attempt an attack; he would bide his time. He felt a foot kick his own and heard words being spat at him in a native tongue that he'd yet to master.

Groaning, he pretended to stretch and looked up at the two men in front of him. He gulped noisily when he saw that one of the men was brandishing a large machete. The man's toothless grin broadened when he saw the fear leap into and settle in Tony's eyes.

* * *

By the time they reached home, both of them were exhausted. Lorne turned to Katy. "Why don't you stay the night, and then travel up first thing?"

Katy pondered for a while and then nodded. "Makes sense. It's a good three-hour drive from here, and I'm knackered."

"Good. That's settled. I'm sure Charlie would love to meet you anyway." She glanced at her watch. Six thirty. "Tom usually drops her off at around seven. Any preference for dinner?"

Katy faced her and frowned. "I'm not fussed. Whatever suits you."

"Well, Friday night is take-away night."

"Really? You eat a lot of take-aways, don't you?"

Lorne cringed. "As a matter of fact, I never used to. I was always having a go at Pete for not eating healthily. I feel a bit of a hypocrite now. It's a time issue. When I was married to Tom, he cooked all the meals during the week, and I took over at the weekend. I'm finding it a struggle to get into a routine, especially with what's happening at the moment—you know, with Tony."

"Lorne, you don't have to make excuses or justify anything to me. I completely understand. Does Charlie like Indian?"

"Does she ever! Actually, it's her favourite, providing it's not too hot. She generally has a chicken tikka. Talking of which, Tony took me to this Indian restaurant once in Oxford, near the river, and the chicken tikka was to die for. All the way through, I sounded like Sally in *When Harry met Sally*—you know the scene I mean. God, it was gorgeous. I must look up the name of the place again. Maybe Tony and I will take a trip out there again when he comes home…"

Katy stroked her arm to comfort her. "Be brave, Lorne. I'm sure he'll return home soon."

"I'm sure you're right. I'm glad I have you for company right now. Have you had any thoughts on your own situation?"

Katy's cheeks blushed a light pink. "Not really."

Lorne smiled and gently nudged her in the ribs. "You and AJ seemed to be getting on well today."

Katy's cheeks turned from pink to beetroot in no time at all. "He seems nice enough."

"Just a word of warning: you know how the force looks on relationships starting up between officers. If anything were to happen between you, I'd hate to lose one of you. Enough said on the subject."

Katy tutted. "We spent the morning together on a case, that's all."

Lorne's eyebrows rose at the way Katy bit back. "I'm just saying." She put her hand on her chest and continued, "If it were up to me, I would say go for it but keep your distance at work. You're less likely to raise suspicions with the other members of the team."

Katy looked shocked. "Are you saying what I think you're saying? That you wouldn't mind if we started something?"

"Hey, look at it this way." She held her hands out in front of her, palms upwards. "Hmm… Darren or AJ?" She lifted one hand, then the other. "It's a no-brainer, in my book."

"You're incorrigible. But AJ is kind of cute—a ladies' man, granted—but ever so cute," Katy admitted, picking up the menu Lorne had dug out of the kitchen drawer.

A satisfied grin settled on Lorne's face as she prepared Henry's evening meal of biscuits and tinned beef.

"As soon as you've decided what you're having." Lorne laughed before clarifying, "Take-away-wise, I mean. We'll ring through the order before they get busy."

Katy ran her finger down the list and back up again until she finally picked out the lamb bhuna.

Lorne rang the restaurant and placed the order, adding her own dish of chicken korma to Charlie and Katy's orders. Not long after, the doorbell rang, and her weekend began.

After the meal, while Katy packed her bag, Lorne stretched out on the sofa with Charlie tucked up in front of her.

"Mum, I'm stuffed now…"

Lorne knew her daughter well enough when something was puzzling her. "What's up, love?" She swept her daughter's mousey brown hair back from covering her eyes.

"Dad told me about Tony. He'll be back for the wedding, won't he?"

At first she was annoyed that Tom had told their daughter, but before doing him an injustice, she asked, "What did Dad tell you?"

"Only that he'd been called away. Dad wasn't sure if he'd be back for the wedding or not." Charlie turned to face her. "What's going on, Mum? We've been through so much together. I know when something isn't right."

Lorne tapped her daughter on the nose, then squeezed her tight. "You're a perceptive munchkin. He's on a mission. Hopefully, he'll be back soon."

"But he's been on missions before, Mum, and you haven't had those worry lines that I'm seeing now."

"I know, sweetie. Put it down to a tough week at work, Tony being away, plus all the preparations I'm having to do for the wedding."

Again Lorne found herself surprised by Charlie's perceptiveness when she persisted. "But you've got a wedding planner to organise that for you, haven't you?"

Lorne sighed and smiled at her. "When did God make you so smart, young lady?"

Charlie chuckled. "He probably gave me your brain genes instead of Dad's."

There was no doubting that, as Tom had shown over the years that he wasn't and never would be the sharpest knife in the drawer.

"Going back to the wedding, we need to sort out a dress for you. We should've done it a while ago, but I needed to get the renovations finished before I went back to the force."

"Aww… I was hoping you had forgotten about that. Do I have to wear a dress? Couldn't I wear a nice trouser suit or something?" Charlie whined with a pleading look.

Trying to avoid a teenage strop that could ruin their weekend, Lorne told her daughter, "We'll see. What about a compromise? We'll go to the bridal shop. You try on a couple of dresses. If none of them take your fancy, we move on and look for a trouser suit for you."

"I guess, that'll be all right. Does the dress have to be a pale colour?"

"Not necessarily. What about a red one? You could wear it to parties in the future."

Charlie screwed her nose up. "I wouldn't be seen dead in a dress at a party."

Lorne laughed as she remembered the tussle she'd had in her teens with her own mother, when she had tried to force Lorne into a party dress for the first time for her cousin's eighteenth birthday. It had been raining, and she and her parents had decided to walk to the party, which was being held a few streets away. Her mother had bought her some strappy sandals with two and a half–inch heels that matched her pink blancmange dress. In a mood from having her hair curled and pinned up in an elegant bun, Lorne hatched a plan to spoil her dress and shoes in one go. Seeing a large crack in the pavement she intentionally wedged her heel in it, and when she tried to walk on pretended to lose her balance and ended up in a muddy pool of water in the gutter.

Aghast, her parents had whisked her home to change. In the end, she attended the party in the outfit she had wanted to wear initially, much to her parents' disappointment. She had no intention of making Charlie go through the same ordeal. After her daughter's excruciating experience with Baldwin, her discipline had become more lax. Charlie was more of an adult than a normal girl her age, something Lorne still felt guilty about.

"Mum… Earth to Mum."

Coming out of her reverie, she kissed her daughter on the forehead. "We'll see what happens at the bridal shop. Deal?"

Reluctantly her daughter agreed, and they settled down to the latest rom-com video starring Cameron Diaz.

* * *

The following day, after waving Katy off, Lorne and Charlie headed to Sam's house. Lorne looked in the rearview mirror and watched Henry sitting in the back seat. One minute, he was sitting erect panting excitedly; the next, when the car turned into Greenacre Road, his head dropped. He knew exactly where he was going and what it meant. Her heart went out to him as another bout of guilt swept through her. After working all week and leaving him in the house alone, she owed it to him to be there at the weekend, but she also owed it to Charlie to spend time with her, too. It was a no-win situation.

"It's only for the day, boy. You'll have fun with Grandpa."

Charlie turned in her seat and patted Henry on the head. "I'll take you for a long walk tomorrow, boy, and a run in the park. How's that?"

His ears pricked up at the 'W' word, and he barked in response, which eased Lorne's guilt slightly.

A couple of hours later, they had reached the rink and were busy fastening up their skates.

"You look petrified, Mum." Charlie laughed and stood up on the rubber matting that led onto the rink entrance.

"No, I'll be fine. Apprehensive but not petrified."

Tentatively they stepped onto the ice. Lorne almost immediately fell on her backside, much to her daughter's delight. Determined, she got to her feet, took a few seconds to steady herself and ran the skates back and forward, getting the feel of them. Sucking in a breath, she watched as Charlie, skating like a junior pro, came around to join her.

"Come on, Mum. Get a move on. Our time will run out soon."

"Oy, you cheeky mare." Leading with her right foot, she pushed away from the side. At first, her legs felt like they belonged to someone else, but then the rhythm began to feel like second nature to her. Within fifteen minutes and after a few falls, she was skating like she had in her teens, with confidence and elegance.

"Wow, Mum. Look at you go." Charlie came up behind her, and they skated together side by side, holding hands.

After their jaunt on the ice, they headed upstairs to the café and ordered toasted buttered teacakes and mugs of hot chocolate before setting off for the bridal shop in the heart of the city.

Charlie tried on a couple of dresses, as promised, but even Lorne had to admit they didn't suit her child one bit. Lorne searched the rails and spotted a mid-blue linen two-piece suit that she thought would go well with her daughter's colouring. She took it into the changing room where Charlie was just slipping out of the final dress she'd tried on.

"What do you think of this?"

Her daughter poked her head out of the cubicle, and her eyes widened in delight. "That's stunning. Can I try it on?"

"Of course. I think it's beautiful. It'll match some of the flowers I've ordered, too."

"I'll be two minutes," Charlie called out excitedly.

A confident Charlie stepped out of the cubicle a few minutes later. Proud tears sprang to Lorne's eyes. The suit was a perfect fit and enhanced her daughter's burgeoning beauty.

"Oh, darling. It's beautiful... You're beautiful."

The shop's owner, a little Italian lady in her early-forties, appeared and uttered one word. "*Bellissima.*"

"Sold," Lorne said, smiling at the woman.

It wasn't until Lorne passed over her credit card that she realised how expensive the suit was. Still, she knew Charlie would get years of use out of it. In the end, £250 was a snip. She just hoped Tony would agree.

Arm in arm, they left the bridal shop. Lorne had another surprise up her sleeve for her teenage daughter as they headed for one of London's newest landmarks.

"You're kidding me?" Charlie shouted joyfully as they walked towards The Eye, one of London's newest and most popular tourist attractions. Lorne had been promising the trip for the past couple of years, but something had always cropped up, pushing the trip back.

"Come on; hop on." The trip was well worth the exorbitant price as they surveyed the London skyline that was just starting to light up against the backdrop of the dusky sky. Lorne pointed out the other landmarks, most of which Charlie knew, but some she hadn't heard of before.

"This is the best day ever, Mum. It's a shame Tony isn't here with us."

Lorne swallowed down the lump that suddenly appeared in her throat and threw her arm around Charlie's shoulders. "I know, love. There'll be other trips when he can join us," she said, more to reassure herself rather than Charlie.

They ate at an expensive restaurant that evening, and when they got home, they both stumbled into bed.

The next morning, Lorne woke up invigorated after having one of the best night's sleep she'd had since the news broke about Tony. Breakfast consisted of scrambled eggs on toast with streaky bacon on the side, one of Charlie's personal favourites. A couple of games of Scrabble filled their morning before Lorne headed into the kitchen to prepare lunch.

The doorbell rang at twelve thirty. Charlie jumped up. "I'll get it!"

"Put the chain on before you answer—" Lorne knew her words had fallen on deaf ears when Henry bounded into the kitchen before she'd had time to finish her sentence.

Lorne crouched down and hugged him. He moaned and licked her face, letting her know he was pleased to see her. "I missed you, sweetie. Guess who's going to get spoilt today?"

"He's spoilt every day of the week," her father said from the doorway.

"Yeah, and I bet you spoilt him rotten yesterday too, old man."

Acting as though he'd been caught out, he mumbled indignantly, "I did not."

Charlie joined them and wrapped her arms around her grandfather's waist. "Yeah, Mum's right. You always spoil him. I've seen your stash of doggie treats in the cupboard under the stairs."

Her father cringed, and Lorne laughed. "Oh, is that right? You hypocrite!"

"Telltale." Sam Collins smiled adoringly at his granddaughter. "Oh, and you know that stash of sweets I have in my kitchen cupboard for when you visit? They're going in the bin the minute I get home."

"I don't believe you. You wouldn't do that to your favourite grandchild," Charlie challenged.

Shrugging and grinning broadly, he told her, "We'll see how nice you are to me today. You've got a lot of making up to do, miss."

Charlie and Lorne exchanged knowing glances as they prepared the table for lunch. After they had devoured the roast pork dinner and a syrup sponge pudding and custard, everyone collapsed in their chairs, patting their full stomachs. Lorne made a mental note to buy some salad the next time she went shopping to help shed some of the calories she had put on that week. The last thing she wanted to do when Tony got home was look like Porky Pig.

By seven that evening, the house was quiet, and Lorne was relaxing on the sofa with Henry, her cheeks aching from smiling and laughing too much during the day. She was just summoning up the effort to get out of the chair and go to bed when the phone rang. She retrieved it from the side table beside her and answered it. "Hello?"

"Lorne, it's Patti."

Lorne could tell by the tone of the pathologist's voice that she had bad news. "Hi, Patti. Go on, hit me with it."

"Are you sitting down?"

"I am."

"I've just had a quick communication with Dave. It lasted seconds—that's all, Lorne, so don't go getting worked up about what I'm going to tell you, okay?"

Lorne ran a hand through her hair and prepared herself for bad news. "Go on."

"Dave told me they're aware of where Tony is—"

"My God, is he all right? I'm sorry, please continue, Patti."

She heard Patti expel a breath before she went on, "They're monitoring the situation, Lorne. Apparently, he's in a cave being guarded by a large group of men. That's all Dave said before the line went dead."

"Oh, Patti, I'm so grateful to you both. It's the not knowing anything that's eating me up. I know you probably can't answer this, but do you suspect they'll try a rescue attempt?"

"I'd say that's a given. They tend to closely survey situations for a few days rather jump in feet first. The last thing I want to do is get your hopes up, but to me the news sounds positive. I just wanted to make you aware at the earliest opportunity."

"I can't thank you enough, Patti. I've been going out of my mind with worry, obviously. At least this news gives me something to latch on to."

Lorne could hear the smile wipe away the worry in the other woman's voice when she replied, "That's why I thought I'd ring you straight away. Try and get some rest now. I'll speak to you soon."

"Thank you, I will. I appreciate your call. Good night."

The first thing Lorne did was tearfully relay the news to her father. When she hung up, Henry sat in front of her with his head tilted to the side. Flinging her arms around him, she gave him a bear hug; and with tears running down her cheeks, she whispered, "Daddy's coming home, sweet pea. He's coming home."

Chapter Twenty-Two

Lorne breezed into the incident room the next morning with a huge grin lighting up her face.

Katy was already there; she must have left Manchester in the early hours of the morning to get there by nine. She followed Lorne into her office. "You've heard good news, I take it?"

Lorne nodded and swept a casual hand through her hair. "I can't really tell you, but I have had a snippet of information, yes."

Sitting down, Katy smiled. "I'm so pleased for you."

"Hey, enough about me. How was your weekend? I hope Darren didn't pop up."

"No, thankfully. He did call, though. I've told him we're finished and I want him to get his stuff out of the flat immediately."

"Good girl. How did he take the news?"

Katy's mouth twisted. "The way I thought he would. Called me all the names he could think of and said it wasn't over until he said it was."

"Oh, is that right? That young man is forgetting you're a copper, isn't he?"

"Selective memory, I think it's called."

Lorne laughed. "Hold firm. For what it's worth, I think you're doing the right thing. Once an abuser, they rarely break the cycle in my experience, both personal and professional. It's all about power. If you stand firm and show him he no longer has the power over you, he'll soon give up."

She hoped that would be the case with Darren, although in her time on the force Lorne had seen several abusive relationships end up with the abuser behind bars, serving a life sentence for killing his partner because of his unwillingness to relinquish the power he had over his spouse or girlfriend. She would do anything in her power to ensure that Katy's relationship didn't come to that. If that meant another warning in Darren's ear, then so be it.

"What's on the agenda today, boss?" Katy asked, swiftly changing the subject.

Lorne flicked through the pile of post on the desk in front of her. "Actually, I thought we might return the files to the security firm today. I know we didn't find much, but I thought we'd make them think the opposite."

"Sounds good. What time do you want to set off?"

She waved the letters in her hand. "Probably take me a good half an hour to get through this lot. Gather the files together for the security firm and the designer. We might as well drop those back too, while we're at it, or pretend too. I'd like to keep the pressure on these guys."

Katy left the office, and Lorne picked up her phone and called her superior. "Sir? Just a quick one to say that I've had some tentative news about Tony."

"Is he all right?" Roberts asked, concerned.

"I can't say much at the moment. Let's just say the news has come as a welcome relief."

"Thanks for keeping me informed, Lorne. We'll catch up on the case later. I've got a meeting with the super in a few minutes."

"I'll be out this morning putting the squeeze on a few suspects. Hopefully be back some time after lunch."

"We'll catch up then."

* * *

Lorne pulled the car into the car park of the security firm a couple of hours later. When she pushed open the front door, she was surprised to see only one person present.

"Is Mr. Underhill around?"

His assistant, who had raised his head and seen them walk in, kept his eyes on the paperwork in front of him. "Nope."

"Where is he?" Lorne tried not to grind her teeth.

"Called in sick." The guy rudely avoided looking up at her when he answered.

"Does he call—" Lorne slapped her hand on his paperwork, grabbing his attention.

"Jeez, lady! You scared the shit out of me."

"Your customer relations suck. Now give me your full attention. Does he call in sick often?"

The young man shook his head. "This is the first time since we started up."

"Give me his address," Lorne ordered, her suspicions churning. "Don't look at me like that. Hurry up."

He jotted down the address quickly, and the two detectives ran out to the car.

"What's wrong?" asked Katy as Lorne put Underhill's address into the Sat Nav.

She put her foot down, leaving a trail of dust behind her as she exited the car park before responding. "Don't you find it odd that he should give us a name one day and not turn up for work the next?"

Katy shrugged, picking up on her meaning. "I suppose so."

After arriving at Underhill's address, Lorne noticed that the curtains were drawn. She rang the bell on the mid-terraced cottage and stood back to see if the curtains twitched. They did. Lorne gave the man a few minutes to answer. When he neglected to, she kept her finger pressed on the brass doorbell for a count of ten before letting go. Still no answer.

Calling through the letterbox, Lorne warned, "If this door isn't opened within thirty seconds, Mr. Underhill, we'll break it down."

Counting in her head, she made it to twenty-seven before they heard the chain being unlatched. The door creaked open barely two inches and a croaky voice asked, "What do you want, Inspector?"

Not liking how the man sounded, Lorne gently pushed against the door and gasped when she saw the state he was in. It looked like the trip downstairs had sapped all his strength. Leaning against the hall wall, his head back and knees bent, Underhill groaned noisily.

"Katy, quick! Help me support him."

With the detectives either side of him, almost carrying him, they eased their way down a narrow hallway and into a monochrome lounge. They lowered Underhill into a brown leather sofa and stepped back.

Her heart went out to him. Both his eyes were black and doubled in size and his nose was clearly broken. He had a patch of first-aid gauze taped to his right ear, but the blood had seeped through and turned the material deep maroon. He was partially clothed; his trousers were covered in blood, too. Lorne guessed the blood was from the injuries to his face and ear, but it didn't stop her being concerned that he'd suffered further injuries to his legs.

Lorne reached forward and lifted his vest up. His whole stomach was rainbow-coloured. "Ouch! Philip, who did this?"

His swollen, shaking hand moved gingerly to his vest and tugged it back down. Through thick lips, cracked in several places, he croaked, "I can't tell you."

"You have to tell me." Turning to Katy, she ordered, "Go and find me a jacket and a shirt, will you?"

She watched Katy leave the room with her head down, deep in thought, and wondered if the sergeant was thinking of her own predicament and how it could've been her looking like this. Whoever had beaten Underhill black and blue meant business, not a warning. The attack was a 'You screwed up big time' message, with an underlying threat that the next time he said or did something out of place, he'd end up in the mortuary.

Lorne perched on the sofa beside him, placed a finger under his chin to make him look at her. "We can get you help, Philip. Put you in the witness protection programme if need be."

Pulling his chin from her grasp, he shook his head—gently, as if he feared the damage a more vigorous effort might entail. "It's because I spoke to you in the first place that I'm in this mess."

That was all she needed to know. Rising from the chair, Lorne left the room and called the station on her mobile.

"AJ, it's me. Drop what you're doing. I want you to go and pick up Zac Murray for me. Take a couple of uniforms with you for backup."

"Okay, ma'am. Am I picking him up for questioning or what?"

"Questioning at the moment for GBH. We're at Underhill's house, and Zac's given him a pasting. Let me know when you've got him."

"Yes, ma'am. I'll get onto it straight away."

"And, AJ? Let DS Fox know that we're on our way to the hospital. We'll be back ASAP."

"Will do. Be in touch soon, I hope."

Katy came down the stairs as Lorne flipped her phone shut. "Are you all right?"

"Better than him, anyway," Katy said, nodding her head in the direction of the lounge. "Any idea who did it?"

"Yep, Zac. I've just rung base to bring him in."

"If they can find him. What's the betting he's gone underground?"

Lorne exhaled, turned to walk back into the lounge, and muttered, "I hope for Underhill's sake, he hasn't."

Chapter Twenty-Three

After spending most of the afternoon at Accident and Emergency with Underhill, the two detectives returned to the station. The minute she walked into the incident room, Lorne could tell AJ was about to deliver some bad news.

"AJ?"

He shook his head and said regretfully, "He wasn't at home, ma'am. We don't have a workplace listed for him either. We searched the area and asked around, but no one had a clue where he was or where he hangs out."

"It's a long shot, but did you try the pub? The Cross Keys, I mean?"

By the time she was halfway through her question, he was already nodding and looking dejected.

She thumped her thigh and slumped down on the edge of the desk behind her. "Okay, issue uniform with his description. I want him tracked down ASAP. He's the key to this case. That much is evident."

"Will do. Umm... The chief wanted a word when you returned."

She pushed off the desk and headed up the hallway to Roberts' office. Margaret nodded for her to go straight in, and Lorne gave a brief smile in return before she entered the office.

"Ah, Lorne. How's it going?"

"Slowly. I believe Zac Murray battered the bloke at the security firm for talking to us."

"Did he say that?"

"Not directly, no. He was too scared to. He did tell me he was in enough trouble for talking to me already. My assumption is that Zac paid him a visit."

"Is it serious?"

"After sitting in A&E with him, they took him down for surgery. He has a couple of busted ribs and fibula. Plus a broken nose and cheek bone."

"Someone meant business, then. Will he talk if we assure his safety?"

Lorne shrugged. "I'm not sure. I tried the hook of the witness programme, but there wasn't an ounce of interest. Can't say I blame him, really. The programme has had some bad press recently, hasn't it?"

"I suppose you're right. Is the team out looking for this Zac?"

"They've just returned. Been out there for a good three or four hours and drawn numerous blanks."

"I'm sure he'll turn up soon, and when he does, we'll be waiting for him."

Lorne raised her eyebrows. "Are you sanctioning overtime, sir?"

"If it means getting a violent criminal who sounds like he's a loose cannon off our streets, then yes."

Surprised, she turned to leave.

"Just one thing before you go, Lorne."

Recognising the tone of his voice, she swung back to face him. "Sir?"

"How are you holding up?"

"Fine. To be honest and not wishing to sound heartless, I've pushed Tony's situation to the back of my mind, now that I know he's being looked after. Sort of."

"You know where I am."

"I know and I appreciate it, Sean. I'm sure Tony will be home soon. And I'm also sure my team will track Zac Murray down soon, too. I'll let you know what happens."

"Two officers on an overnight stakeout. Let's see what results that brings us."

Pushing through the swing doors to the incident room, she shouted, "Volunteers for overtime!" A couple of the regular officers, always on the lookout for extra pay, raised their hands. She decided to go with someone more senior and pointed at AJ first. "Thanks, AJ. Knew I could count on you. John, do you fancy the graveyard shift?"

At first Fox pulled a face, but upon reflection, he nodded his agreement.

She glanced at her watch. "It's just after four now. Why don't you two go home for a couple of hours and meet back here at, say, nine?"

John and AJ both slipped on their jackets and left the room. Lorne returned to her office and rang DI Holland.

"Steve. I'm on the lookout for Zac Murray. Can you get your guys to keep an eye out for him?"

"Sure. What's he done?"

"GBH, I think. He beat up one of the people we're investigating. The thing is, I can't issue a warrant for his arrest, as the victim refuses to name him."

"Hmm… Tricky. I take it you've offered the victim protection."

Lorne nodded as if he was in the room with her. "Yeah, but he's not snatching my hand off to take it. I wondered if you had any other background information you can give me on him? You know the type of thing, details or hearsay that never make it to the computer."

"Hang on. Let me bring up my personal file on him. We've all got one of those, right?" He laughed.

Lorne waited a few seconds as he tapped the keyboard before she specified, "The type of thing I'm looking for is family ties and maybe bother with other gangs. Either inside or outside of prison."

She heard his fingers hit the keys faster. Had she jolted something in his memory?

"Here it is. He got into a scrap inside. One of my guys was investigating this other gang at the time. Bob Denman. Maybe he's the guy you saw in the pub the other day."

Lorne described the man in the pub while he pulled up another file on his computer.

Sounding pleased with himself, Steve reeled off the information he'd found. "Bob Denman, another petty-stroke-borderline hard criminal. He and his gang have been on the rob for years. I remember now—Murray had a brother. He was the top man. Something happened to him… Now, what was it?" Holland laughed. "Too many bloody criminals vying for attention in my brain at the moment. Can't for the life of me recall what happened to him. Anyway, this Murray—the brother—and Denman go back years, rival gangs. Like I say, it was always just petty stuff."

"That's brilliant, Steve. It gives me something to go on, at least. This case is bugging the life out of me, and I want it sorted before any other murders are committed."

"Hey, any time, kiddo."

Lorne left her office and started jotting things down on the whiteboard in the incident room. Within half an hour, she had all the players, everyone who had cropped up so far—including the designer Danielle Styles—noted on the board. Now all she had to do was start joining them up.

"Molly, can you start delving into Zac Murray's background? AJ didn't come up with much when he searched, but he might have been looking in the wrong direction."

"Ma'am? I'm not sure what you mean by that. AJ's research is always thorough."

Lorne held her hands up apologetically. "Sorry, I'm thinking ahead of myself here. It wasn't a slight on AJ's skills. What I meant to say is, instead of looking directly at Zac Murray, look around him—family, friends, *et cetera*. He's the key to this, either directly or indirectly."

"I see. I'll get onto it straight away." Molly sounded relieved.

"Katy, come here, will you?"

A bemused Katy stepped forward and stood beside her.

Her eyes still directed at the board, Lorne asked her new partner, "What do you see?"

Katy took a few moments to study the board before she shrugged and replied, "Nothing much. Let me rephrase that: nothing more than we had already, ma'am."

"You're right, Katy, and *that's* what is so bloody annoying. The pieces just don't match yet. Let's hope John and AJ catch Murray tonight."

"There's a call for you, ma'am," Tracy shouted across the room.

"Who is it?"

"It's Mr. Dobbs." Tracy sounded disheartened.

"Put it through to the office, Tracy, will you?" She ran into the office and slammed the door behind her.

"Hello, Mr. Dobbs. How's your wife?" The man's sobs took Lorne's breath away and made her think the worst.

Then he managed to pull himself together long enough to say, "They're putting her in a psych ward."

"What? Why? Mr. Dobbs, please try and tell me what happened," she coaxed gently.

"I only left her for a moment. She was eating, see, and…"

"And what, Mr. Dobbs?" Lorne coaxed urgently.

"She slit her wrists with the knife."

The news devastated her. They had lost so much. The husband and wife needed to stick together as a united team, with their children's funerals coming up.

"I'm so sorry. Is she all right? Did Trisha regain her memory?"

The man cried openly as he forced out the words. "She hadn't, no, until a family member let it slip about the kids... She'll never be the same again. The guilt is just too much for her to take. For me to take... I want our kids back."

"I know it's difficult, Dave, but you have to remain strong, for both your sakes. The doctors will take good care of Trisha. I'm sorry you're both having to go through this."

He remained silent for a few moments. "Tell me you'll get the bastards who did this, please? I have to live with this god-awful pain and guilt for the rest of my life, our lives. It won't bring my kids back... but I need to know the bastards who destroyed my family will be brought to justice."

"You have my assurance, Mr. Dobbs. Again, please accept my apologies for what you're having to go through. I'll keep you informed as and when we have any news. Take care."

Lorne replaced the phone and thumped the desk with her hand. *How dare these bastards rip that family apart like this! How dare they!*

Chapter Twenty-Four

Lorne had insisted that Katy should stay the night with her, after the sergeant had beaten the sunrise by a few hours that morning and carried out a full shift at work.

The following day, they arrived at work early, at a quarter to nine, to the news that Zac Murray had been in a cell all night and was ready for questioning.

Lorne punched the air and patted AJ and John on the shoulder. "Good job, guys. Why don't you go home for a couple of hours? If things go the way I want them to, I'll need all hands available later on today. That's *if* Murray starts squealing."

The two men left, and Katy followed her into her office.

"I'm going to let Murray stew for another hour or so. Arrange for a duty solicitor to attend, will you? Can you gather the information I asked Molly to collect for me? I'll take a quick look through that before I tackle him."

Katy left the office and returned with a manila folder with Zac Murray's name on it and placed it on the desk in front of Lorne. "The solicitor is booked for ten. Molly said she couldn't find much on Murray, but there are a couple of snippets of information in there that she thinks will prove to be interesting."

"Thanks. Do me a favour and get me a coffee." She reached into her coat pocket and threw a fifty pence piece on the desk.

Looking insulted, Katy turned on her heel and walked out of the room, reappearing almost instantly with two cups of coffee. "That's the least I can do after you putting me up. Umm… I thought I might go home tonight, if that's okay with you?"

Surprised, Lorne sipped at her coffee, then said, "It's up to you. The offer is still open to stay while Tony is away, remember that. Will Darren be around?"

"I hope not. I told him to collect his stuff. That's why I need to go home, really, to see if he's done it."

Katy half-smiled, and Lorne could tell she was apprehensive. "Would you like me to come home with you?"

The sergeant waved her hand in front of her. "Nah, I'll be fine. You've got enough on your plate already, plus we don't know how today is going to pan out yet."

"If you're sure," Lorne said, before teasing, "We could always ask AJ to accompany you."

Katy's cheeks coloured slightly. "Crikey, don't you dare. Can you imagine how that would look if Darren were there?"

Lorne smirked. "Yeah, it'd be good, wouldn't it?"

Both of them laughed. "You're wicked. What do you want me to do?"

"I'd like you to sit in on the interview with me. Until then, if you can, have a word with the team, see if they've managed to dig anything else up. Also, gather the crime scene photos for me, will you? All *three* scenes."

"On my way."

Watching Katy leave, Lorne picked up her phone and called Roberts. "Good news, I hope."

Sounding interested he said, "Go on."

"The overtime paid off. AJ and John managed to locate Murray. He's in a cell. I'm going to start questioning him in an hour or so." While she was talking, Lorne opened the file Molly had collated and scanned the pages.

Hmm... That's interesting.

"Inspector?"

"Sorry, boss. What did you say?"

"I said 'Let me know how the interview goes.' Actually, I asked if you could remember how to interview a suspect, but I changed my mind." Roberts chuckled.

"Charming! I'll take that remark with the contempt it deserves. I'll keep you informed, sir."

She hung up and searched through the file some more, making notes in her notebook as she went. A little while later, she rang the desk sergeant to check if the solicitor had arrived. When the sergeant told her he had, she asked him to prepare an interview room and to transfer Murray to it within the next five minutes.

"You ready?" Lorne asked Katy as she slipped her notebook into the jacket pocket of her black business suit.

Picking up the file containing the crime scene photos, Katy nodded. Lorne couldn't help noticing how troubled she looked, so on the way downstairs, Lorne pulled Katy to a halt. "What's wrong?" If she hadn't known any better, she would've said that Katy had reverted to the way she was last week when she'd first joined the team, burrowed deep in her shell.

Katy sucked in a deep breath and tried to give her a reassuring smile. "I'm fine. Seeing the photos again affected me for some reason."

"It's been a long week for both of us. I know this is going to sound harsh, but you do get used to it. I know we shouldn't, but working on the murder squad, you have to get used to seeing horrendous pictures pretty darn quickly. It goes with the territory, I'm afraid."

"Oh I know that, ma'am. It was just seeing the kids again, that's all. How can the poor parents go on, knowing that their children died like that?"

Lorne shrugged. "That's going to be the hardest part of all, as the Dobbses are finding out at this very minute. And that's why we have to get in there and tease the information out of Murray. DI Holland reckons he's one of these types that needs to be told what to do. Well, there'll be no one holding his hand in there—apart from the duty solicitor, that is. Let's give it our best shot, eh?" Lorne held up her hand, and Katy gave her a high five. "Come on. Copy me and shake all those negative feelings away."

They both continued descending the stairs while shaking out their extended arms, much to the amusement of several uniformed officers passing by. One of them threw a cheeky comment over his shoulder, and Lorne shouted back at him, "Up yours, Cartwright."

Lorne checked with Katy that she was up to the interview before they entered the room. After receiving the sergeant's reassurance, they marched confidently into the room.

The duty solicitor was someone Lorne recognized, a gaunt-looking man in his early forties who had a receding hairline, by the name of Tyler. A uniformed officer stood in the corner behind Murray's chair.

Katy sat in the chair opposite Tyler while Lorne took the chair across from Murray. He looked rough, with dark rings surrounded his sunken eyes and his hair sticking up as if he'd spent the night running his hands through it and trying to pull it from its roots.

Lorne turned on the tape and said the usual required details: the time, date, and who was present in the room. "So, Mr. Murray, how do you know Mr. Underhill?"

Murray eyed her with contempt. His eyes sparkled with amusement, and the left side of his lips lifted into a sneer, and the words Lorne expected tumbled out: "No comment."

Lorne persevered with the nice cop routine for the next fifteen minutes and received the same response over and over. She took out her black notebook and dropped it on the desk. It was time to up the stakes. Startled by the noise, Murray jumped slightly, but his eyes never strayed from his hands, which were interlocked on the table in front of him.

With her pen, she tapped just in front of his hands. "You have some pretty nasty abrasions on your hands, Mr. Murray. Care to tell me how you got them?"

Instantly, Murray scooped his hands back and folded his arms, hiding his marked hands under his armpits. "No comment."

Nonchalantly, she opened her notebook and said nothing for the next few minutes, just turned the pages back and forth a few times. Glancing up, she noticed the solicitor shaking his head and smirking as he made notes on his A4 pad.

"Okay, here's the thing, Zac. I'm going to get the police doc to take a sample from your cuts, and if Underhill's DNA shows up—" She clapped her hands together loudly, making Zac jump for a second time. "Bingo! The evidence will be handed to us on a plate. So?"

The suspect snarled at her. "You think you're so clever, don't ya?"

Frowning, she asked, "What makes you say that, Zac? Come on. Admit the GBH, and then we can move on."

"I ain't admitting to nothin'." A hate-filled smile stretched his lips into a thin line across his yellowing teeth.

"I'm sure your brother would be urging you to accept the charge if he was here."

A momentary, confused look flittered across his pale face. "Don't get ya."

"Trevor, isn't it?"

The solicitor and his client exchanged nonplussed glances before Tyler said, "Inspector, I'm not sure what my client's brother has to do with this. Are we still talking about the GBH charge?"

Out of the corner of her eye, Lorne saw Katy writing in her notebook, which she passed over to Lorne. The note read: *Now you have him by the short and curlies.*

"Excellent point, sergeant," she said, stifling a grin.

A determined Tyler tried to grab the notebook from Lorne's hand, but she pulled it back out of his eager grasp.

"I demand to know what you two are up to." Tyler sat upright in his uncomfortable chair.

"How many brothers do you have, Zac?"

"One. Trevor."

"Ah, right. It must have been a distressing time for you when he went missing."

Zac's confusion increased. "Yeah, it was. But…"

And with that one word, she knew that Zac had just dug himself a six-foot hole. "But?"

Under the table, his trainers scuffed the concrete floor, and he started to fidget in his seat under her cool gaze.

Mumbling, he said, "I didn't say *but*. You misheard me."

She looked over at Tyler. "Did you hear your client say 'but,' Mr. Tyler?"

He nodded.

"*But*. Such a small word *but* a vitally important word, nonetheless." She started writing it over and over on a spare page in her notebook to emphasise her point. "My friend told me an interesting fact about you the other day, during my enquiries."

"What?" he snapped defensively.

"In connection with another case I'm working on. You'll see in a moment where the pieces fit. My friend told me that you're the type who needs to be led. Is that right, Zac? Is someone pulling your strings?"

"What the fuck are you on about?"

If ever a suspect looked rattled, it was him. She was enjoying the look of panic that had settled in his eyes and pushed on. "I'm asking you again, Mr. Murray, what is your connection with Philip Underhill?"

"No comment."

"Okay, let me put it this way—make it simpler for you, if you like. I believe your brother Trevor is alive." She paused to gauge his reaction. "And that you and your pal Carl Ward are behind some robberies I'm investigating."

Tyler chirped up, "Now wait just a minute, Inspector. My understanding is that my client has been brought in for questioning regarding a GBH charge. I know nothing about any robberies, and neither does he."

"That's strange, Mr. Tyler. How do you know your client doesn't know about the robberies? Just because *you* haven't been privy to the information doesn't mean Zac here knows nothing about them."

Murray spoke next. "I know nothing about any robberies."

But, as his eyes looked over to the left, Lorne knew he was lying. "Did Trevor tell you to beat Underhill up to stop him from talking to us?"

"Nope," Murray told her as his eyes dropped down to her notebook.

"Ah, so you admit Trevor is alive, then?"

"I didn't say that."

Tyler shook his head again and eyed his client with frustration. Lorne held back a snigger that was dying to escape. "Here's my take on things, Zac. Correct me if I'm wrong as I explain things, won't you?"

Murray remained silent, so she continued. Katy pushed the folder in front of Lorne, and one by one, she placed the pictures of Rebecca and Jacob Dobbs on the desk before the suspect. She heard him gulp noisily and knew the pictures had affected him. Then she picked up the pictures of Lewis Kelly lying dead on his bed and thrust them before him.

"While footballer Dave Dobbs was playing a match last Tuesday evening, you, Carl, and a third person—whom I suspect was your brother Trevor—broke into their house. Only you didn't actually have to break in, did you? You'd already made sure that Underhill's security firm made it easy for you to enter the property. How am I doing so far?"

Zac's jaw hung open.

"For the tape, Mr. Murray's jaw is open, and he has a shocked look on his face. I'm reading that to mean that so far, my assumptions are pretty accurate. I'll continue. So, who's idea was it to kill the kids, Zac? Yours?"

"No, it fucking wasn't. I'd never…"

Feeling smug, Lorne raised her eyebrow at the solicitor, who had started to look disinterested in defending his client's inept reactions to the questioning.

"You'd never *what*, Zac? Slit a child's throat like this." She snatched up the photo of little Jacob Dobbs and held it in front of Murray's face. "He was *two*. What could a two-year-old do to harm a man of your size?"

"I'm sorry," he mumbled under his breath.

"What did you say, Mr. Murray? Please repeat for the tape?"

But he refused to, so she twisted the screws further. "Why did you leave Mrs. Dobbs alive?"

He shrugged.

"That woman will have to live with the image of her children being murdered by you and your gang for the rest of her life. Here's a snippet of information for you: I received a disturbing call yesterday from Mr. Dobbs. His wife had tried to commit suicide. The guilt has proved to be too much for her. How's *your* guilt holding up? Whose idea was it to kill the kids? Trevor's?"

He angrily thrust his hands through his ginger hair as a pained expression twisted his face.

Instead of waiting for him to answer, Lorne struck again, searching out his jugular. "So what's it to be, Zac? Take the rap for GBH, or shall I hit you with a murder charge? Actually, make that all three murders."

Murray's head whipped round to Tyler in desperation, but the solicitor kept his eyes focused on his pad and refused to make eye contact with his client. When Murray looked at her, she noticed his eyes were watering.

"Are they tears of guilt or desperation, Zac?" she asked sarcastically.

He wiped the wetness from his eyes with the back of his hand and snapped back, "Neither. I told you: I ain't done nothin' wrong."

Lorne bashed her flattened hand down on the desk and coolly said, "And I'm telling you that you *have*. Mr. Underhill has already said that when he's well enough, he's going to come in and tell us your involvement in all of this."

"Ha! That means he's going to implicate himself, then," Murray said, foolishly walking into the trap she had set for him.

"I've heard enough. DS Foster, get the duty sergeant in here and get him to place Mr. Murray under arrest." Lorne scraped the chair on the floor as she stood up.

"Wait… You can't arrest me without proof. I know my rights."

"Yeah, and I know mine, too, Murray. You either cooperate or..."

His shoulders slumped in defeat, shaking his head, he mumbled, "I can't."

"Can't what?" Lorne asked, taking her seat again.

Murray clammed up. And again Lorne rose from her chair and headed for the door. "Very well. If that's the way you want to play it. I'll leave you with this warning, Murray." She held her hand up and placed her thumb and forefinger an inch apart. "I'm this close, thanks to you slipping up during the course of this interview, to putting all the pieces together. I have every confidence, once we have Underhill's statement and we collect his DNA from your wounds, that your brother and Carl Ward will be residing in a cell near you shortly."

He gave a derisory laugh. "Good luck with that one. My brother's been missing for three years."

Lorne laughed and said to Katy, "Maybe we ought to play the tape back to Mr. Murray to refresh his memory about what he's told us over the last hour."

Katy reached for the tape but paused when Murray, looking confused, scratched his head. He opened his mouth to speak but closed it almost immediately.

Lorne left the room thinking she was at last on the right track, and it was only a matter of time before the case drew to a satisfactory conclusion.

Chapter Twenty-Five

Once back in the incident room, Lorne waited a few minutes for Katy to join her before she started issuing instructions.

"Okay, here's where we stand. While AJ and John get some sleep, I want the rest of you to delve into three people's pasts for me." She walked up to the board and circled three names. "Molly, what you pulled up on Trevor Murray was brilliant, but I need more. What occupation did he have before he disappeared? Any contacts, family members, wife or girlfriend. Did anyone gain from his 'supposed disappearance,' for instance?"

"I'll get on it right away, ma'am."

"Tracy, I'd like you to dig into Carl Ward's past. From what we've learned so far, he and Zac Murray have been involved in petty criminal activities for a few years now. Go back through his record; see when he was first arrested. I want to know who his employer was before he got into trouble. Any wife or girlfriend in the picture, *et cetera*. We have to find some kind of connections. I'm sure we've taken one of the main players out of the equation, so I don't anticipate any more robberies. My guess is people will be spinning around on the spot, not knowing which way to turn."

"I'm on it, ma'am," Tracy said, already tapping away at her computer.

"Katy, I'd like you to dig into Danielle Styles' background, friends, family, *et cetera*. Where did she get her money from to start such a business? What qualifications has she got to call herself an interior designer? I'll be in my office. The minute you find anything, let me know ASAP."

She called Roberts as soon as she entered the office and filled him in on what an idiot Murray had been during the interview.

He laughed. "Sounds a bit dense. Maybe Holland was right about someone having to pull his strings. What are you planning now?"

"I'm wondering if I should do a news conference," Lorne replied.

"Yep, I think we should. Greenfall was asking why we hadn't done one before now. I used Trisha Dobbs' condition as an excuse— you know, losing her memory and not being told about her kids.

Now that she knows, we need to get something organised. Would you like me to handle it?"

"That would be one thing less for me to worry about. I've got a lot on my plate—or I *will* have, in the next few days."

"Such as?" Roberts queried.

Lorne picked up her pen and tapped it on the desk. "I've got the girls researching three people I suspect have a huge part in this. John and AJ have taken the morning off. Hope that's okay?"

"Of course. They did well. Go on."

"I thought this afternoon and tomorrow I would visit the designer again, then the Kellys' friend, and this Denman."

"Denman?" Roberts queried.

"The guy Murray had a scuffle with in the pub. DI Holland seems to think there's some kind of history between Denman and the Murray gang."

"That's fair enough. Now, don't take this the wrong way, but I'd feel better if AJ accompanied you when you tackle Denman."

Lorne bit down on her tongue and sucked in a breath, releasing it slowly before she answered, "Are you saying that Katy and I wouldn't be able to handle him?"

"Inspector, you know I would never insinuate that. I just think it makes sense for a male officer to go with you. I don't have to remind you that you've been off the force for two years, do I?"

"No, sir, you don't. But I still don't get where you're coming from." She thought back to how she'd successfully handled Katy's boyfriend Darren without much bother. The trouble was that DCI Roberts wasn't aware of that particular event, and she had no intention of telling him.

It was Roberts' turn to exhale. "Lorne, since you've been away, the gang culture has escalated considerably. Please don't fight me on this one."

Reluctantly, she accepted his point of view. "Okay, you win. But if Katy kicks off, I'll be pointing her in your direction for the answer."

"If you must. I've got a meeting to attend. Keep me informed."

"Don't I always?"

He neither agreed nor disagreed before he hung up. It wasn't every DI who contacted their DCI with every course of action taken to solve a case. Lorne did because she and Roberts had agreed that she would until she eased herself back into the role of DI. *A bit of moral support never hurt anyone, did it?*

Lorne booted up her computer and started searching for results on Bob Denman.

Half an hour later, she had noted down his home address, but she struggled to find much else about him, except that he had made most of his money from being a property developer. She could understand that. There was good money to be had in renovations, as she knew full well. She thought it would be best to bring Denman in for questioning that afternoon, providing she and AJ could track him down.

A knock on the door broke into her train of thought. "Come in?"

"I've just had an alert, ma'am." Tracy handed her a sheet of paper.

Lorne took in the information, and a light bulb went off in her head. "This could be great news, Tracy. Thanks. Will you send DS Foster in, please?"

Tracy nodded and left.

"You wanted me?" Katy walked into the office and sat down.

"Yep. Tracy's just handed me this." She passed the sheet of paper over the desk. "Could be something important. Some of the Dobbses' jewellery has shown up at a pawnbroker's. Maybe Carl or Trevor Murray tried to fence it when they heard Zac had been picked up."

"You think?"

Frowning, Lorne asked, "You don't?"

Katy's mouth turned down. "I find it hard to believe they would have heard about Zac yet. It's too early."

Lorne thought about that for a minute or two. "You're probably right. I suppose it has been a week since the robbery; it could be a coincidence. Something we'll have to look into, anyway. Right. This afternoon, I'd like you and Tracy to go question the Kellys' friend, Kim Smalling." She watched as Katy's head tilted and her eyebrow rose. "I'm going to see Denman. I'll be taking AJ with me."

"But…"

"I'm under instructions. Sorry, Katy. Don't take it personally. I'm sure the DCI has insisted for my benefit, no other reason." Lorne's take on the situation seemed to appease Katy, thankfully.

"No problem from my end. It'll be good to get to know the other members of the team. Tracy seems eager and willing to assist me."

"Carry on delving into Danielle Styles' past. Hopefully you'll be able to use some of that as ammunition when you visit Smalling. She's a friend of Styles', isn't she?"

"What are you going to do about that?" Katy asked, nodding at the sheet of paper.

"I might call in to see the pawnbroker before I go over to Denman. They're not too far apart. About twenty minutes, I think."

Katy stood up. "I'll get back to it, then. Shall I order in some sandwiches for later?"

"Good idea. Straight after lunch, we'll see whose cages we can rattle and who spills what first."

Chapter Twenty-Six

When Lorne and AJ arrived at the pawnbroker's at five minutes to two, the shop was shut. A Day-Glo orange sign at eye level told any prospective customers that the proprietor was out to lunch and the shop would re-open at two.

"We'll wait in the café on the corner. If he sees us waiting outside, he might think again about opening up on time."

AJ bought them both a cup of coffee. At the table, Lorne stared out the window at the shop. "You and Katy seem to be getting on well. She's a nice girl."

"Yes, ma'am." AJ gave a brief nod.

"I've warned Katy, and now I'm warning you, AJ. Be careful. There are several reasons why you shouldn't get involved, the main one being your careers. You're both going places. I'd hate to see anything jeopardise that." Lorne glanced at him and smiled when she saw the slight colour change in his cheeks.

"Message received, ma'am, but—"

Just then, a Merc pulled up outside the barred door of the shop. A rotund man in his early sixties hoisted himself out of the passenger seat, and the car, driven by a woman half the man's age, left.

"Here we go."

They finished their drinks and walked across the street to the pawnbrokers. The bell rang to announce their arrival. A voice out the back hollered, "Be with you in a minute."

The shop was a mess. Apart from the glass display cabinets in front of them that were in some semblance of order, everything else appeared to be haphazardly thrown on the shelves. Videos and CDs were piled on top of each other with the plastic case edge showing instead of the titles. Every few feet or so, a toaster sat on the shelf, most of them scratched to pieces and belonging in a skip.

Lorne found it hard to believe that anyone would target the shop to try and steal any of the crap on sale, so why the bars on the door and windows?

The man came through the jangling beaded curtain and stopped dead when he saw them. Recovering well, he moved behind the counter, placed his hands on the glass, and gave them one of the falsest smiles Lorne had ever encountered. "What can I do for you nice folks?"

Flashing her warrant card, Lorne asked, "Are you Mr. Boskins?"

He ran a nervous hand across his brow and over his balding head. "That's right. Something wrong?"

Lorne held his gaze. "We have it on good authority that you have some jewellery for sale here that was reported stolen last week."

Boskins looked physically sick by that piece of news. "Now, wait just a minute. Anything that comes in my shop is legit."

Lorne turned to AJ and asked, "Did I insinuate anything in my question?"

AJ shook his head, playing along with her. "Not that I know of, boss."

"If that's the case, you won't mind showing us your books, then, Mr. Boskins. Will you?" Lorne gave a sugar sweet smile.

"Not without a warrant." The man pushed back his shoulders and puffed out his chest.

Lorne remained quiet for a moment, and her gaze dropped to the glass cabinet before her, she turned her head this way and that and pointed at a necklace. "AJ, isn't that the necklace that was stolen from the house where those two kiddies were murdered?"

"Hmm... Sure looks like it to me, boss."

"What? I know—nothing about—any murders," Boskins stammered. He kicked out at what sounded like a cardboard box behind the counter.

By his reaction, Lorne had a feeling he was telling the truth. "Been told some porkies, have you?"

"You have to believe me. I had no idea. This guy dropped the stuff off, and I bunged him a couple of hundred quid for it."

The second that someone said, 'You have to believe me,' Lorne smelled a rat. She suspected the sum he'd mentioned was far from accurate. "You expect me to believe that, Mr. Boskins?"

"Believe what you like. It's the truth." He sneered.

The shop's phone started ringing. He went to answer it, but Lorne told him to leave it. "I'd like to get to the bottom of your involvement in this. Therefore, I'd like you to accompany us to the station."

"What? Why? I buy and sell stuff, that's all. I don't know what I'm buying half the time. Most of my punters are stoned out of their minds when they come in here. Pawning their old gran's stuff just so they can buy some more drugs. I tell you, I know nothing about any kids dying."

"Really?" Lorne asked, cocking an eyebrow.

"Yes, *really.*" He raised his voice. "I've got grandkids of my own. The thought of—"

"If the thought abhors you that much, then you won't mind giving us a name, will you?"

The man paced up and down a number of times before he slumped down on a stall at the end of the counter near the window.

"If I give you a name, can we come to some sort of deal?"

"I'm listening," Lorne said, suppressing a smug smile.

He shook his head. "Assurances before I open my mouth."

Lorne nodded. "I agree. Give me the name and the jewellery. I've got no qualms with you, Boskins. I just want the bastards who killed those kids."

"Carl Ward and Zac Murray."

"Just the two names?" Lorne asked. The way the man's gaze evaded hers spoke volumes. He was obviously keeping back another name, but she was prepared to let it go. For now. "Thank you. Now the jewellery."

He expelled a deep breath. "I shifted the gear abroad. This was the only piece I kept. Stupid, I know, but I thought this piece would go better over here. They deal more in eighteen carat over there. This is only nine."

"Okay. Does the name Bob Denman ring any bells?" Lorne asked, watching intently for any kind of recognition when she mentioned the name. She saw Boskins shuffle a little and decided to proceed with her questions. "I can see it does. Deal with him much?"

Boskins gave a defeated shrug. "A little."

"What can you tell me about him?" Lorne took out her notebook. She flipped through a few pages until she came to the notes she'd made on Denman.

He lifted his shoulders again. "His boys bring me gear now and then. Nothing much."

"He brings you tat, is that what you're telling me?"

"If you like. I wouldn't put it that way to him, though." He laughed, but under Lorne's glare, his smile vanished.

Her pen poised, she asked, "Had anything recently?"

"How recent?" Boskins asked

"Has his gang brought anything in this past week?"

Boskins nodded.

"Like what?"

"Nothing much. Just some costume jewellery. I passed it over to a friend of mine who runs a small shop in Islington."

"I'll need the name of your friend."

"Dora Fields. Hey, she ain't dodgy. She's cleaner than a bleached toilet. I'll tell you what... if you want the goods back, I'll get them for you. Leave her out of this, yeah?"

As Boskins seemed to be cooperating, Lorne nodded her agreement. "Very well, then. How often does Denman bring you gear?"

"Depends. Not that often, really."

"Is Denman friendly with Ward and Murray?" Lorne knew the answer, which made it a good question to test the water and see how truthful Boskins was being.

He snorted. "You're kidding, aren't you? After what happened..."

Lorne looked up from her notebook and frowned. "Don't stop there. Why don't you fill me in?"

"Not sure I can give you specific details. I can only tell you the gossip I heard. I never heard it from the horse's mouth, as such."

"Go on. We're listening."

Before they left the tacky shop, Boskins had told them of the hassle between the two gangs. Gossip was that both gangs had independently come up with a plan to rob a post office, but the Murray gang had been the one to make off with the cash. Rumour had it that the haul was a couple of hundred grand. So petty criminal Zac Murray wasn't so petty after all, or maybe his brother was the one who got his hands dirty on that job.

It was time to tackle Denman about the post office job and the third robbery, the one that hadn't ended up in murder. Lorne was now confident Denman's gang was behind that, and the Murray gang had carried out the other two robberies. It wasn't a case of a copycat crime, but a 'one-upmanship crime' involving the same security firm.

* * *

Trevor Murray answered his mobile and almost immediately held it away from his ear. "What the fuck are you playing at?"

"Hold on, Boskins. What are you going on about? Have you fenced that gear, yet?"

Boskins growled down the phone. "Fuck your stuff and fuck you in the future, Murray, you dick. If I'd known you'd killed those kids, I would never have dealt with you in the first place. You're sick!"

"All right, old man. Climb down off your fucking merry-go-round horse. What's brought this on?"

"You prat! You take everyone else for fucking idiots, when you were at the bottom of the pile when they were handing brains out."

"What are you going on about?"

Boskins scratched his balding head out of frustration. "The cops have been here. They told me what you did to them nippers. In the future, fucking take your knocked-off gear elsewhere, you hear me?"

Chapter Twenty-Seven

Lorne got out of the car and whistled. The art deco–style mansion house was set in its own grounds at the end of a tree-lined drive. A tacky plastic-looking nude fountain, out of keeping with its surroundings, graced the driveway about twenty feet from the front door.

"Nice place for a petty," she said out of the corner of her mouth as AJ yanked on the ornate brass bell chain to the right of the front door.

"Apparently, crime does pay," AJ replied, shaking his head.

The door opened, and the man recognised Lorne immediately. His welcoming smile slipped momentarily and was replaced by an angry glare before it swiftly reverted back.

Amused, Lorne asked, "Bob Denman? Mind if we come in and have a chat?"

"About what exactly?"

The two officers flashed their warrant cards and moved forwards at the same time. Denman took the hint and swept his arm back, inviting them in. A German shepherd approached them, wagging its tail, and sniffed each of the detectives in turn.

"Rex, leave it. Go lie down," Denman ordered tersely. The dog moaned and retreated down the vast hallway.

The inside of the house wasn't a patch on the outside. Lorne loved the Mackintosh-designed wallpaper in the hallway, but wasn't all that keen on the stepped design furniture littering it. It just looked as though someone had said, 'Yes, this is art deco. We'll furnish our house with it, lots of it.' Lorne's keen designer instincts, developed over the last few years, told her that the house would benefit from a 'less is more' perspective for the design element to work well.

Denman showed them into a large, open-planned L-shaped living room–cum–kitchen. Again Lorne couldn't help screwing her nose up. The setup was far too modern for a house built in the thirties. The work had tarnished the house's integrity.

"Can I get you a drink? Tea or coffee, I mean, of course."

"No thanks. We've got a few questions to ask, if you don't mind. Now that I've managed to track you down, Mr. Denman."

He motioned for them to take a seat on the black leather sofa and sat down in the single-seater opposite them.

Lorne held his gaze. Before entering the house, she had told AJ to take notes throughout the meeting. "Now, where do I begin? Ah, yes. How about the last time I saw you? At The Cross Keys last week."

His brow furrowed, and his eyes narrowed—not obviously, just enough for Lorne to notice. "The Cross Keys? I'm afraid I don't remember."

"I thought you might say that." She took out her mobile from her coat pocket and trawled through the photos. When she found the one she was looking for, she handed it to him. "Maybe this will refresh your memory."

At first he refused to take the phone from her. She waved it around in front of him until he backed down and snatched it from her grasp.

He briefly glanced at her phone. "All right. I'll admit I was there. What do you want to know?" He abruptly returned her phone.

"I want to know what went on between you and Zac Murray?"

He thought about his answer for the briefest moment. "Not sure what you're getting at, Inspector."

"Mr. Denman, either we can do this the easy way, or we can talk about this down at the station." She stood up. "In fact, why don't we do that?"

Denman reclined back in his chair and started swivelling it from left to right. "Now, don't be hasty, Inspector. You can't blame a man for trying."

He gave her a smile that turned her stomach. She detested men who thought all they had to do was smile at a woman to have her twisted around their little finger. *Arsehole!*

"We haven't got all day, Mr. Denman." Lorne tapped her foot.

He raised his hands then dropped them again. "Let's call it unfinished business."

"What '*unfinished* business'?" Her tone was bored, and he raised an eyebrow at her. "The fact that your gang and the Murray gang got in each other's way on a job once?"

"Someone been telling tales, have they?"

"I couldn't possibly say, Mr. Denman. Why don't you tell me your side of the story?"

His right shoulder lifted up to his ear. "There's really not that much to tell. I had a little…" He cleared his throat. "Let's say business transaction, but Murray and his numbskull pals balled it up for me."

"So, in the pub last week, you threatened him?"

Acting like an innocent schoolboy, he flattened his hand against his chest. "Moi! I'm not in the habit of threatening people for a living, Inspector."

"Really? And what exactly do you do for a living that warrants a grand house like this?"

"This and that." One side of his mouth curled up into a snide grin.

"Does 'this and that' extend to burglary?"

Feigning puzzlement, his gaze drifted out the French doors to the garden for a moment, then returned to her. "Not sure who told you that, but they were wrong."

"I don't think so. I have it on good authority that you and your gang were very active last week."

His confidence looked as though it had temporarily been knocked off its axis. His tongue slipped out and moistened his dry lips as he contemplated his reply. Lorne gave an imaginary thump in the air. *Get out of that one, you smarmy shit!*

"Have any proof of that, Inspector?"

"We're working on it." She decided to have some fun, to try to corner him the way she had Murray. "With three crime scenes to go through for evidence, I expect the results on my desk within the next few days." She saw the lump slide down his throat, and he slipped a finger around his starched collar, loosening it as if it was constricting the life out of him. "Something wrong, Mr. Denman?"

Although he cleared his throat, his voice still came out croaky. "No. I know nothing about any burglaries, let alone three of them."

Not satisfied, Lorne ventured further. "Here's the thing: Whoever carried out these crimes will be looking at long stretches."

He frowned. "Has the law changed or something? Since when did burglaries carry a long stretch?"

Lorne stood up, went over to the French doors and looked out at the landscaped garden, beyond the terrace to the rear of the property. She let him stew for a second or two before she turned around and came to a standstill alongside his chair. He glanced up at her.

"Burglaries don't. But murders do."

Denman flew out of the chair to confront her. AJ jumped up from his seat, but one warning glance from Lorne made him hold back.

"What murders? Burglary in the singular, maybe, but not three of them, and definitely not murders. I would never allow my boys to do that."

She smiled but said nothing as he paced back and forth in front of her. It was as she had suspected; two separate gangs had carried out the crimes. Now all she had to do was find the elusive Murray.

"And Trevor Murray would?"

He shrugged. "I don't know. You'd have to ask him."

"Any idea where we can find him?"

Regaining some of his composure, he said, "What am I, his keeper?"

"Sarcasm isn't really going to help, is it? All I'm asking is have you seen him or have you heard anything on the grapevine about his whereabouts of late?"

"No. After the accident, I hadn't heard a dicky bird until last week."

"And what provoked that verbal assault on Zac Murray, may I ask?"

"All right, I'll give. But you've gotta promise me you'll put in a good word for me." Lorne nodded, so he continued, "One of my guys happened to be in the pub at the same time Underhill and Murray was having a little chinwag. They looked pretty cosy, and when I heard, it rattled me."

"Why? What has Underhill got to do with any of this?" She had a rough idea but needed to be sure she was moving along the right lines.

"He was at the pub one night, drunk, mouthing off about who his clients were and that he was going places."

"I see… And?"

"I had a quiet word with him, offered him a backhander if he turned the system off for a while. At first, he wanted nothing to do with the plan, but I could see his little brain cells working overtime. It wasn't until I offered him a cut of the haul that he agreed. I don't like being double-crossed, so when I heard of Murray and Underhill meeting up, I sussed what was going on."

"What, that Underhill knew he was onto a good thing and thought he'd offer the service around to other criminals?"

"Yep. He's a tosser. I should've known not to trust the bloody weasel. 'Trust Us,' my fucking arse. I should never have got into bed with him, so to speak."

"Do you think Underhill knows where Trevor Murray is?" Lorne was infuriated that the 'weasel' had managed to dupe her and even made her feel sorry for him. The time she'd wasted at the hospital to ensure that his injuries were properly taken care of stuck in her throat.

Denman shook his head. "I doubt it. I keep my ear to the ground, and I've not heard anything about Murray."

"We're going to have to ask you to accompany us to the station. I appreciate your help, but you've admitted that you carried out the robbery on the Kendrickson's home. Are you going to come willingly, or do I need to get my partner to cuff you?"

"There's no need for that."

"I'll need the names of the rest of your gang, too." Lorne had her mobile in her hand poised ready to call the information in.

"I'm no snitch. I'll take the rap."

Lorne laughed, finding his statement ironic, and walked towards the front door with Denman and AJ behind her. At least one part of the case had been solved.

Chapter Twenty-Eight

After leaving Denman with the desk sergeant to be charged, Lorne and AJ returned to the incident room. By the looks of things, Katy and Tracy, who were still wearing their coats, had not long returned themselves.

Slipping out of her coat, Lorne asked, "Everything all right?"

Katy made her way over to the board and started drawing lines to connect the suspects' names. "Here's something you'll find interesting, boss."

Intrigued, Lorne joined her and watched as she drew a line from Kim Smalling to Carl Ward. "What's the connection?"

"Boyfriend and girlfriend," Katy replied, looking pleased with herself.

Lorne nodded. "Really? Now that is interesting."

Katy shook her head. "They were. Not any longer."

"Oh, why? Tell you what: Let's grab a coffee, and we can exchange information. AJ and I have just pulled Denman in."

Lorne and Katy stepped into the office, grabbing coffees *en route*. Once settled in their seats, Lorne was eager to hear what the others had found out and told Katy to go first in the reveal.

"Well, bearing in mind that it was just after lunch when we got there, Smalling was in a terrible state, heavily intoxicated. She told me she hadn't slept for almost a week."

"How come?" Lorne asked, sipping her coffee.

"Guilt."

"She's friends with Sandra Kelly, isn't she?"

"That's right. She's supposed to be her best mate. Christ, with mates like her, I'd hate to meet her enemies."

"Sounds ominous. What did she do?"

Katy let out a deep breath before she began. "All she had to do was open her mouth to her boyfriend, and without realising it, she set this whole thing rolling. Yes, she was *best* friends with Sandra Kelly. They grew up together, in the same class throughout school, and even lived on the same road as kids."

"I think I know where this is leading," Lorne said sadly.

"Right. Sandra Kelly got married about four years ago. All of a sudden, her lifestyle changed. She moved into the big house where she now lives, and Smalling felt as though she'd been pushed aside.

Smalling told us that every time she visited the new house, Sandra would show her around and point out everything that she had spent a fortune on since her last visit."

"Ah, envy. It's a pitiful sin. So she told Ward, and he and the Murray brothers robbed the place."

"That's about it."

"Hang on a minute. I seem to remember Mr. Kelly saying that Kim also suggested using the designer."

Katy nodded. "That's right. I think she's also played a key role in all of this."

"So how did you leave it with Smalling, and why did she dump Ward?"

"She's riddled with guilt—at least, that's what she says. But she had no idea they were going to kill anyone. She can't come to terms with the fact that she caused the little boy's death."

"She should feel bloody guilty. What is wrong with these people? Sick shits! So we need to lay a charge of accessory on her, don't we?"

"I'll get a uniform to pick her up, shall I? Tracy and I debated whether to bring her in or not, but we concluded that she was so drunk it wouldn't hurt to leave her a day or two."

Lorne nodded. "Agreed. Let a uniform pick her up tomorrow."

"How come Denman has been brought in?"

Over the next fifteen minutes, Lorne filled her partner in on what had happened at Denman's place and how Underhill was connected to the crimes.

"The sneaky shit. I had a strange feeling about Underhill from the word *go*," Katy said.

"Looks like your instincts were good. Let's call it a day here. I'll drop you back at your house. We'll start afresh tomorrow."

Katy nodded and suddenly looked apprehensive.

Lorne smiled reassuringly. "You don't have to go home if you don't want to."

"I know. If I don't do it now, though, I'll never have the courage to do it."

Chapter Twenty-Nine

When they got to Katy's place, the two detectives got out of the car and dashed across the road trying to escape the downpour as quickly as they could.

"What the hell?" Katy asked when they approached the front door of her flat. The door had been pushed back and wedged open with a large book. Katy picked up her book, turning to face Lorne with tears in her eyes. "My mum bought me this for my eighteenth. It's a book of poetry. Darren knows how precious this is to me."

Lorne tugged Katy back. Armed with her pepper spray, she walked into the flat. The place was an absolute mess. In the lounge, all the chairs had been slashed with a knife. The rest of the furniture had been defaced by what looked to be spray paint, the type used for spraying cars. The graffiti artist's handiwork was evident on all the walls, too.

"Oh shit! Bang goes my bloody five hundred quid deposit. Why would he do such a thing?"

"I'm sorry, love. There's no call for this. I'll take a look in the kitchen and bedroom." Lorne eyed her partner with concern as Katy lowered herself onto the wooden arm of the easy chair.

The kitchen was in an even worse state than the lounge. Every conceivable drawer and cupboard had been emptied, and their contents lay strewn across the ripped lino floor. All the pots were misshapen. Most of the handles had been torn off and discarded in a pile by the bin in the corner.

Jeez, and they say to watch out when a woman is scorned.

Although the table appeared to be intact, the four chairs surrounding it each had a leg or two missing.

As Lorne made her way up the hallway to the bedroom, she heard Katy on the phone. Easing the door open, Lorne found every piece of furniture destroyed, just like in the other rooms.

"You sadistic piece of shit... You know what you fucking did... Don't give me that bullshit... I'm going to press charges... I'm not going to let this rest..."

Katy joined Lorne in the bedroom and gasped. "Oh shit! He didn't do my clothes as well?" She kicked out at the chest of drawers before sinking to her knees to gather up her underwear.

"I take it he's denying he did it?" Lorne asked, her heart heavy with the implications of Katy's whole wardrobe being ripped to shreds.

"Yeah, he did. How could he hate me so much? What am I going to do? How am I ever going to trust another man after this? Do you think that was his intention?"

Lorne shrugged. "I don't know what goes on in someone's mind if they have to resort to this. It's as though he still wants to have control over your life, even if he isn't going to be a part of it in the future."

"How could anyone be so vindictive towards another human being like that?"

Katy was young. She had a lot to learn about life and human nature, the good points and the sometimes very bad points. In her time as a copper, Lorne had seen several instances where people had split up and the family pet had been killed because neither party was willing to let the other have it. The human race could be very cold and extremely calculating at times. Often all sense of rationality went out the window without much provocation.

"You need to call this in, Katy."

She looked up at Lorne, crestfallen, and shook her head. "What would be the point? What evidence have I got it was him? He just told me that he removed his stuff and locked the door behind him."

"You can't let him get away with it. He needs to learn right from wrong. What'll happen next time? If he moves in with someone else, and she ends up dumping him? These things have a habit of escalating if they're not stamped out in time. You wouldn't want that on your conscience, would you?"

Running one hand through her hair, Katy threw the shredded silky G-string she held across the room and stood up. "You're right. I'm not going to let him think he's won. That he has something over me."

Katy dialled 999 to report the incident. They spent the next couple of hours trying to gather anything that was perceived to be salvageable, which turned out to be very little.

It was after nine when they finally parked outside Lorne's house. They got out of the car and went to her door. As Lorne placed the key in the lock, they heard footsteps behind them. She and Katy simultaneously reached for their attack sprays.

The man in the expensively tailored suit held his hands up. "Ms. Simpkins? I need a word in private."

"Sorry, and you are?"

"I apologise. Jonathan Edwards. Perhaps Tony has mentioned me."

It had been a really long day, and Lorne had trouble searching her memory bank for his name. "I'm sorry. Not that I can remember. Who are you?"

"I understand your reluctance to let me in, but I must speak with you immediately." He looked over his shoulder up and down the street, then leaned in and whispered, "I'm Tony's boss."

Her shaking hand left the pepper spray in her pocket and flew up to cover her mouth. Katy held her upright as her knees buckled, and she fell against the front door. Reaching behind Lorne's head, Katy continued to unlock the door and helped her boss inside. Henry ran to greet them, but he halted halfway up the hallway to growl at the man who had walked in, closing the door behind him.

"It's all right, boy. I'll put him in the garden and fix a drink," Katy said.

The man stepped forward, hooked his hand under Lorne's elbow, and settled her on the sofa in the lounge.

"I'm sorry. Forgive me. It's been an exhausting day. Please tell me why you're here. It must be bad news."

"May I?" he asked, pointing to the end of the sofa.

"Of course." Lorne watched the slim, tall, blond man perch on the edge of the sofa.

His hands clenched together tightly so that his knuckles turned white instantly. "Please hear me out. I have good news and bad."

Her heart thundered in her chest as she prepared herself for the bad news. "Go on."

"Okay, here it is. I'm only here because Tony asked me to come and tell you in person—"

"Oh my God, you've rescued him?"

She heard him swallow, and his eyes met hers. "Yes, we rescued him, and he's due home in a couple of days."

"But that's wonderful news, isn't it?"

"Ordinarily, yes."

Katy disrupted the conversation to hand them each a cup of coffee before she left the room again.

With her cold, trembling hands wrapped around the warming mug, Lorne asked him to continue.

"Well, we extracted Agent Warner successfully…"

Agent Warner! What happened to calling him Tony? she thought foolishly. "And?"

"I'm sorry to have to tell you that he's in critical condition."

In slow motion, the mug slipped from her hand. It landed with a thump as the carpet swallowed its contents in the wake of its fall.

"But… I don't understand. You told me you spoke to him."

He nodded. "I must clarify. I didn't actually speak to him myself, but one of the SAS guys passed on the message. His only concern was for you, Ms. Simpkins. He wanted to be reassured that you heard the news personally."

She had trouble forcing the next words past the lump that had developed in her throat. "Please… Tell me what's wrong with him."

"I believe you're aware that he was tortured."

"Yes."

The man shifted in his seat as he searched for the words. His gaze slipped down to the floor when he told her, "The bastards cut one of his legs off."

Tears bubbled and cascaded. She covered her face with her hands, trying to disguise her out-of-control emotions. "My God, no… But he will live, won't he?"

Edwards expelled a deep breath. "Like I said, he's in critical condition."

Her mind fraught with worry and unable to think straight, she asked, "Why?"

Instead of talking to her as if she was some kind of idiot who had just asked the dumbest question, he asked softly, "May I call you Lorne?"

"Of course," she said, wiping the tears away with the coat sleeve that she hadn't removed yet.

"Lorne, when the team found him, he had lost a significant amount of blood. He was transferred immediately to an army hospital at Basra. He briefly regained consciousness, before surgery, just long enough to order—yes, I said *order*—for you to be told in person." He paused, smiled warmly, and added, "It's obvious that he loves you very much."

She responded with a short, abrupt laugh. "I should hope so, we're getting married a week on Saturday. At least, we were."

"I'm sorry, I had no idea."

Embarrassed that Tony hadn't informed him, she said, "It's a quiet wedding, just the family."

"There's no need to apologise." Reaching forward he patted her hand. "I'll tell you this, I've known Tony for years. He'll do everything in his power to make sure that happens. Don't give up on him."

His final sentence had shocked her. "I would never give up on him. Never. Even if the Taliban think they've made him into a lesser man. He'll always be the same man to me."

"I understand. Not every woman would say that. I must be going. I'll keep you informed of his progress."

Lorne showed him to the door and kept hold of his outstretched hand longer than necessary. "I appreciate your candour and the fact that you abided by Tony's wishes to give me the news yourself. Thank you."

"Keep your chin up. You're lucky to have each other."

She closed the door behind him and rested against it for a few moments as his words chased each other round her mind.

"Lorne? Are you all right?"

"I will be as soon as Tony comes home. Did you hear any of that?"

Katy had a cloth in her hand and Lorne followed her into the lounge where Katy started mopping up the coffee from the spilt mug.

"I heard little bits. I heard that Tony has been rescued. I'm so pleased for you."

Lorne sat down heavily on the sofa. Henry stood in front of her and whimpered slightly as he rested his head on her lap. "I'm going to ring my dad. I don't mind you listening, as it'll save me having to repeat myself, but can you keep it a secret at work?"

Katy paused in wiping up the coffee and looked up. "That goes without saying, boss."

Picking up the phone, Lorne blew out several breaths as she dialled her father's number. "Hey, Dad, it's me. Are you sitting down?"

"What's wrong? I'm sitting."

"I've just had Tony's boss here. They've got him, Dad."

"Bloody hell he was lucky. I don't mind telling you I've had a dreadful feeling that he wasn't coming back."

That was typical of her father, to always talk a situation up. To think and talk positively to anyone worried about a situation out of their control, even if he had negative feelings about the matter.

"There's more. He's in critical condition…"

"Oh, sweetheart, I'm sorry. Are you all right? Do you want me to come over?"

"I'm fine, Dad. Just knowing that he's alive and that he'll be home in a couple of days is enough to give me the strength to carry on. No, you stay there. Katy's with me."

Her father remained silent on the other end of the line for a while. Finally, Lorne told him, "He's lost a leg." Katy's head rose up, and Lorne spotted the tears welling up in the sergeant's eyes.

"Oh, Jesus. The bastards…"

"I'm not sure how he's going to cope with that, Dad. Or me for that matter."

"You'll cope, darling, and so will he. You can be sure of that. When's he due home?"

"His boss said in a couple of days. He's had surgery out there at the army base. I better go now. The poor dog is starving. Love you."

"Love you too, sweetie. You'll get through this together. I know you will."

Her father said that, but she heard the doubt lingering in his voice. How many times would Tony and she hear the same thing from family and friends in the coming months or years?

Replacing the phone on its stand on the table, Lorne stood up and started to leave the room, but Katy's quiet voice stopped her.

"I'm so sorry, Lorne."

After touching Katy briefly on the shoulder, Lorne continued out into the kitchen, with Henry close on her heels. She prepared his meal through the mist of tears, horrendous images of Tony lying injured and bleeding to death flashed through her mind. The images continued to fester in her dreams—or were they nightmares?—that night. She even woke herself up several times during the night, crying out her injured fiancé's name.

In the end, she opened one of his drawers, took out one of his T-shirts, and spent the rest of the night with it tucked under her head, the scent of him giving her enough comfort to grab at least a couple of hours' sleep.

Chapter Thirty

The next morning, it was hard to focus on the cars ahead of her through the morning fog that was prevalent that time of year, and the fact that her eyes were painfully sore and puffy from the amount of crying she'd done. During the drive to work, each of them was deep in thought, wrapped up in her own specific domestic problems, conscious that once they clocked on, their professionalism would kick in.

Lorne was surprised to find DCI Roberts in the incident room, awaiting her arrival. He had his arms crossed, and his head twisted and tilted as he studied the information pertaining to the case.

Sneaking up behind him, she whispered, "Everything all right, sir?"

He jumped. "Apart from you scaring the life out of me, you mean?"

"Sorry."

He faced her and lifted one of his eyebrows. "You look rough. Something I should know about?"

"Not here. Do you want to take it in my office? Five minutes I can spare, then I want to crack on with the case." *In other words, don't sympathise with me, as I'm liable to break down. I just want— need—to get on with my job.*

Roberts closed the office door behind them. "What's wrong, Lorne?"

She sucked in a deep breath and blew it out slowly before she replied. "They've recovered Tony."

"What do you mean, 'recovered'? He's not...?"

"Sorry, bad choice of word. No, he's alive, just."

They both dropped into their chairs at the same time. "Lorne, I'm sorry. Can you tell me what happened? That is, if it's not too painful for you."

Painful for her? That was a laugh. What about the pain Tony was suffering? After relaying the information she herself had been told the previous evening, Roberts sat there stunned as the news sunk in.

He shook his head slowly. "My God, I'm so sorry. If there's anything I can do... Hey, you shouldn't even be here."

She held her hands up to prevent him pitying her further. "Sean, don't make me go home. You know I do my best thinking when I'm stressed. Let me do this my way, okay?"

He gave her one of those 'Who am I to question you?' looks and apologised a second time.

"He'll be home in a few days. I might need some time off then, if that's okay?"

"Are you kidding? Of course. You know I'll back you all the way. Where are we with the case, then?"

They both stood up and went back into the incident room, taking up positions at the board.

"Katy and Tracy questioned Smalling yesterday. Turns out she used to be the girlfriend of Ward. We started to make some connections at last. Smalling recommended the designer. We're going out to question her again this morning."

"Okay. Any news on Ward yet?"

"Nope. My feeling is he's up to his scrawny neck in this. I'd like to get a warrant for his arrest."

"You know that without any evidence to back up your theory, we won't be able to get one, Inspector."

"Yes, sir, I'm aware of that. Maybe if Smalling is willing to implicate him, which I doubt." She paused to think for a second or two. "Okay, I'll send a couple of uniforms out to his address, see if they can find him to bring him in for questioning."

"That's a better plan, I think. Anything else you're going to be looking into?"

"I keep looking at the board, thinking we're missing something, but I keep coming up blank. I'll see how it goes with Styles today, then decide where to go from there. What about the news conference? The sooner we get that aired, the better. It might cause Ward and Murray to panic and make a mistake."

"It's taking place at eleven this morning. I have a good feeling that we're getting closer to wrapping this up." Lorne laughed gently. "Something amusing about that?" Roberts asked, puzzled.

"I thought only women worked on gut instinct."

"I'll be sure to remind your father of that the next time I see him."

He had a point. She screwed her nose up at him. "Touché!"

"Seriously, with Styles, start to put the pressure on her. Let's see if she snaps."

She nodded. "That was my intention. No more Mrs. Nice Guy anymore. I want these bastards caught."

"Sorry to interrupt, ma'am," Tracy called from across the room.

"No problem. We're finished here, anyway."

Roberts held a finger up, asking Tracy to give him a second. "I'll get off. Keep me informed, and prepare your team for an influx of calls after the conference."

"Yes, sir. Will do." Lorne headed over to Tracy, who was holding the phone, covering the mouthpiece with her right hand. "What's up?"

"It's the pathologist for you, ma'am."

"Put her through," Lorne shouted over her shoulder *en route* to her office. She entered her office and picked up the phone as she sat. "Patti? I was going to ring you later. What have you got for me?"

"You were? Okay, my news first. We ran a simple DNA test on Zac Murray's blood and Underhill's wounds. They're a definite match, but we'll have to wait for the proper test to come back for it to be conclusive."

"Yes! That's great, Patti. Things are looking up on the case. Pieces are slowly beginning to slot together."

"Brilliant. Those poor kids deserve justice. It was a heartless and heinous crime. Now, why were you going to call me?"

Lorne sensed in the woman's tone that Patti already had an idea what Lorne was about to tell her. Lowering her voice—she'd left the door to her office open in her haste to answer the call—she repeated what she'd told Roberts.

"Crap, that's good news and bad then. I know you probably don't want to hear this right now, but they can do wonders with prosthetic limbs nowadays. I have a contact that can help, should you need one."

Lorne smiled and marvelled at her new friend's willingness to help out a second time. "That'd be great, Patti, when the time comes. I'm not sure what state of mind Tony will be in for a while. I'll be sure to let him know."

"Have you thought about the wedding? Maybe putting it back awhile?" Patti asked tentatively.

"Again, I'm waiting to see what happens when he eventually comes home. I'll let you know how things turn out."

"I'm always here if you want a chat."

"I appreciate that more than you'll ever know. Talk soon."

After hanging up, Lorne went in search of her partner. "Katy, we leave in half an hour. Listen up everyone. DCI Roberts is holding a news conference this morning, so be ready to be bombarded with calls. I don't have to tell you how important it is to treat every call as a possible lead. There's bound to be the odd crank one. We know that. All I'm saying is: sift through any possible tips thoroughly. We know the main players in this case by now, bar one. Let's see if anything comes to light about Trevor Murray. Okay?"

A unison "Yes, ma'am" came back to her as she went back in her office to sort through the pile of paperwork that had miraculously appeared on her desk overnight.

* * *

After finishing the paperwork, Lorne drove to the designer's showroom, and parked the car around the corner, out of sight. If Styles saw them approaching, she might make a run for it.

Lorne turned to Katy. "Tell you what. You go round the back. She might try and leg it. If she does, you have my permission to stop her any way you can."

Smirking, they split up. Lorne opened the front door. The bell chimed, and Styles glanced up at her. She looked worried as she made an excuse to the woman she was dealing with, and slipped through the door to the office beyond the showroom. Up for the chase, Lorne sprinted through the same door, almost removing it from its hinges as she burst through it.

The woman was nowhere to be seen. When Lorne asked Styles' shocked assistant where her boss had gone, the young girl glanced at the rear door and shrugged.

"I'll deal with you later. The charge will be aiding a criminal." The woman suddenly changed her mind and pointed in the direction Lorne was already running in. "Thanks."

Hearing a woman's voice, Lorne opted to creep up to the nearest wall on tiptoes. She couldn't make out what Styles was saying, as she was using a hushed tone. Lorne struggled to hear any names mentioned or what the call was about. She had a rough idea though.

Then Lorne heard Katy's abrupt tone telling the woman to hang up. *Shit. That wasn't supposed to happen. I should have told her to hang back.*

Lorne stepped out from behind the wall. "Ah, Ms. Styles. I'm glad we bumped into you. We have a few questions to ask you. Such as, who were you calling?"

Looking behind Lorne as if searching for an escape route, Danielle Styles shifted in her platform-high heels and shook her head. "No one."

"Bollocks. Excuse my language," Lorne added when the woman gave her a horrified look. "I'll give you two minutes to tell your assistant that you're leaving and to pick up your bag."

Styles looked confused. "What? Why?"

Lorne winked at Styles. "Because I think you'll talk more openly in our environment than yours."

Styles floundered for a moment, giving the impression that she was about to argue, before thinking better of it.

Usually when a suspect was transported to the police station for questioning, they remained silent. Styles was anything but, declaring her innocence and incredulity at the situation. She huffed, puffed, and sighed frequently during the twenty-minute drive, asking on more than one occasion if she could smoke after being adamantly told that she could not. Styles finally folded her arms in front of her and pouted like a teenager.

As intended, when they arrived at the station and the desk sergeant booked Styles in for questioning, the woman started to visibly shake. Just the thought of being in a police station had Styles' type quaking in her high heels.

Standing behind Styles, Lorne winked at the sergeant and told him authoritatively, "I don't want to be disturbed for the next couple of hours."

Nodding sternly, he replied, "Yes, ma'am. I'll make sure of it."

Lorne led the way into interview room one, with a reluctant Styles behind her and Katy at the rear. The duty solicitor, Tyler, was already in the room, waiting for them.

Lorne and Tyler acknowledged each other briefly while Katy unwrapped the cellophane from a new tape and inserted it into the machine. Then she said the usual blurb while Lorne sat opposite Styles, giving her an intense stare. The intimidation had begun.

"So, Ms. Styles, where would you like to begin?"

The woman frowned. "I'm not sure what you mean."

"Come now. We know you're involved in the robberies, so please don't bother denying it."

The woman's head snapped round to her solicitor, who as usual, was focused on the A4 pad in front of him. When he didn't register her, she looked back at Lorne with her mouth hanging open.

"What's wrong, Ms. Styles?"

Her fists clenched and unclenched on the desk in front of her until she interlocked her fingers. Avoiding eye contact, she said shakily, "I know nothing about any robberies."

"For the tape, that statement is totally untrue. Sergeant Foster and I questioned Ms. Styles about the robberies a couple of days ago. Perhaps our meeting has slipped her mind. Has it?"

The woman looked on the verge of having a meltdown. "You're twisting my words, Inspector."

"Am I? I'd hate to be guilty of that. So, in your own words, how do you know Zac Murray?"

Confusion was clear in her face. "Who?"

Frustrated, Lorne tried a different name. "What about Carl Ward?"

The woman's mouth turned down at the sides, and she shook her head vigorously. "Never heard of him."

Lorne suspected she was telling the truth. Exhaling, she asked, "Kim Smalling?"

Recognition filtered her eyes, and Styles nodded. "She's a personal friend of mine, but I've never heard of the two men... Oh, wait a minute. Kim was going out with a Carl. Not sure what his surname is, though."

"Have you been in touch with Kim lately?"

"Not for a couple of weeks. Why?"

"I'll ask the questions, if you don't mind. How do you know the footballer Les Kelly?" Lorne asked.

"He's a client of mine. Actually, I dealt more with his wife Sandra than him."

"And you got the contract from Kim. Is that right?" Styles fidgeted in her seat and glanced down at the table. "Is that right?" Lorne repeated when her question went unanswered.

Styles nodded.

"For the tape, Ms. Styles is nodding. Well, here's the thing: We had an interesting chat with Kim Smalling yesterday, and in her distraught state, she let a few things slip."

That grabbed the woman's attention. Styles glanced up at Lorne, her eyes wide with alarm. "Such as?"

"Where do I begin? Zac Murray, Carl Ward, and Trevor Murray—those are the names that cropped up, along with yours. So you'll forgive me if I don't believe you when you say you've never heard of them."

"I corrected myself and told you I had heard of Carl Ward, but I've never met him. And I've definitely never heard of the other names."

"You see, that's what I find hard to believe. From the second I stepped into the Kellys' home after dealing with the murder scene at the Dobbs' house, I had an inkling we were looking at a team. Thanks to Kim, who put all the final pieces together for me, I can now start arresting people and charging them with murder."

Styles stood up and knocked over her chair, pointing at Lorne, she said, "I had nothing to do with any murders, and I'm not going down for them, either." She prodded Tyler in the arm and added, "Say something. Tell her I had nothing to do with this—not the murders, anyway."

Lorne held back a smile when Tyler spoke. "Sit down, Ms. Styles. You're making a damn fool of yourself. Just tell the Inspector what she wants to know, and we can all get out of here."

Defeated, Styles picked her chair up and slumped into it. "I know nothing about the murders," she repeated, angrily. "I refuse to be held accountable for any of that."

Tilting her head, Lorne asked calmly, "So what was your part?"

"I don't really know how I got mixed up in this. Honestly, I don't."

"I'll be the judge of that. Now, tell me what you know."

Moistening her pink lipstick–coloured lips, she began, "Kim told me her boyfriend was planning to rob some footballers' homes. She's friends with the Kellys and wanted to know who else was worth robbing. They knew that most of my clients nowadays are wealthy footballers. I gave them a list, but I felt bad about doing it. Kim said I owed her for putting the work my way in the first place."

"Go on. Was there anyone else involved?"

Styles remained quiet for a while, and Lorne could tell she was torn about whether to answer the question or not. She pushed the woman again for an answer. "It'll be to your benefit to tell us, Ms. Styles."

The woman blew out a long breath and looked at all the people around the table in turn before she said, "Stuart Russell."

Lorne tossed the name around in her mind for a few seconds, but it didn't ring any bells. "Stuart Russell?"

Styles sat forward in her chair, resting her elbows on the desk. She supported her head in her hands.

With reluctance, Styles repeated the name. "Stuart Russell. He helped me set up my business. A silent partner, if you like."

"Ah, the business you're not qualified to run, you mean." The woman looked stunned by the news. "We do our research thoroughly, Ms. Styles. Any reason you gave up your course at college?"

Shrugging, she sat back in her chair again. "I got bored. I met this Stuart a couple of years ago. He said I had talent. He offered to back me if I set up a company. He even put some clients my way."

Lorne saw the woman cringe when the final words were out. "What *aren't* you telling me?"

Styles sighed heavily. "Stuart Russell is an agent."

Perplexed, Lorne asked, "An agent? For what?" Then it dawned on her where she'd heard the name before.

Chapter Thirty-One

The interview came to an abrupt halt. After instructing Katy to get down Styles' statement, Lorne bolted into the incident room. She approached the evidence board and shook her head in disgust. She knew the information had been in front of her all along, but other things had steered her away from the one person she should have questioned right from the start.

AJ walked up and stood beside her. "Everything all right, ma'am?"

She thumped her clenched fist against her thigh and faced him. "No, it's not." Stepping closer to the board, she tapped her finger on the name that she knew would haunt her for years to come. "Stuart Russell. Why the heck haven't we questioned him yet?"

"Are you saying that he's got something to do with this?" AJ asked, looking shocked.

"Okay, enough farting around. Get his address, home and office. We'll take a ride out there to see what he has to say."

While the sergeant sorted out the information, Lorne rang DCI Roberts.

After filling him in on the details, she said downheartedly, "Sorry, sir. I messed up."

"Not sure how you work that one out, Inspector. Do you want me to organise some form of backup?"

"I don't think that will be necessary. Let's see what he has to say first. I'm so bloody annoyed with myself."

"It's understandable after all you've been through."

"Please don't try and make excuses for me. I should have spotted—"

"You can make amends now. It's not too late, Lorne, and definitely not worth beating yourself up about. Let me know how it goes." With that, he hung up.

Lorne was left feeling grateful that he hadn't shouted at her and chastised her incompetence. If her commanding officer had been anyone else, she knew that would have been the case. *Enough self-pity. Crack on, and bring him in.*

* * *

The personal assistant was out of her chair like a shot when Lorne and AJ swept past her and into Russell's office.

The man in his early forties studied Lorne with what appeared to be amusement. "Did I miss this appointment in my diary, Lizzie?" he asked the outraged blonde holding onto the door.

"No, sir. They barged in before I could stop them."

Lorne flashed her warrant card at the secretary, then Russell. The secretary gawped at her ID, but Russell seemed to be unperturbed, which made Lorne even more suspicious of the man sitting confidently behind his oversized desk.

"Got time to squeeze in a little chat with the police in your busy schedule, have you?"

His smile broadened, and his eyes sparkled mischievously. "Never been one to not help out the police when I can. Mind if I ask you what this is about?"

Lorne noticed the way his pen picked up speed as he wound it through his fingers. She opened her mouth to speak, but he raised a hand to stop her. "Can I get you any refreshments?"

"No, thanks. We won't be long," Lorne responded curtly.

"That'll be all, Lizzie," he said, dismissing the furious secretary. He pointed at the chairs in front of them, but Lorne and AJ remained standing.

Lorne said, "Over the last couple of days, we've had some pretty interesting conversations."

He gave a derisory laugh. "I'm sure you have, in your line of work."

There was no fooling Lorne. She noticed the nervous twitch at the side of his mouth. "Care to tell me how you know Danielle Styles?"

"Why?" he retorted a little too sharply.

"Just answer the question, please."

"The young lady has talent." When Lorne cocked an interested eyebrow, he clarified, "As an interior designer, I meant."

"How long have you known each other?"

The smile had slipped from his tanned face, "I guess a couple of years. Is she in any trouble?"

Ignoring his question, she asked, "Is it right that you're a silent partner in her business?"

"That's right." Another short, curt reply.

"Can I ask why?"

His brow furrowed. "I'm not sure what you're getting at, Inspector."

"Why did you decide to invest in her company?"

"It was a business opportunity that I couldn't pass up. Is there a law now against investing money that I haven't heard about?" he responded.

Lorne held his gaze for several seconds and soon concluded that he was a very cagey character. "Are you sleeping with her, too?"

At first, he appeared taken aback by the question, but he recovered quickly to admit, "We might have been bedfellows at one time. Do you mind getting to the point of this intrusion, Inspector?"

"The point is that we're from the Serious Crime Squad. We're investigating a couple of robberies and believe that you and your lady friend have something to do with the crimes."

His temper momentarily flared up but soon died down again. "In what way?" he asked, calmly.

Lorne moved to the chair and sat down. AJ followed her. "Come now. Don't tell me you have no idea what I'm talking about." Shrugging, he pulled a 'So what?' face. Lorne decided to play along with him for a while. "Tell me, how long have you been a football agent?"

"A couple of years."

"And before that?" she asked.

"I had several businesses."

"What *kind* of businesses exactly?"

Leaning back in his chair, he folded his arms. He obviously worked out regularly, by the way his suit pulled across his upper arms. He slightly screwed up his eyes for a brief second. "Mostly I dabbled in stocks and shares. But when the market collapsed, I had to invest my money elsewhere. Hence my partnership with Danielle."

"I'm confused. So what experience do you need to be a football agent, then?"

"A smart brain and the gift of the gab, most of the time," he said, laughing.

"Ah, I see. Yes, I can tell you're a master of that." Her words didn't seem to offend him in the slightest. If anything, he seemed to take the mild insult as compliment. He was beginning to piss her off.

"So, perhaps you can answer me this, then. What do you do to earn your vast fee?" She surveyed the plush office to make her point. Everything was still glistening as if it was all totally brand new.

"I look after the players' needs, mainly, and negotiate good deals on their contracts."

Puzzled, she tilted her head and asked, "Look after their needs?"

"That's right," he replied, giving very little away.

Not satisfied with his response, she pushed him further. "Give me a rundown of what your day entails, will you? Just so I have it clear in my mind how important your role is."

Lorne spotted a couple of beads of sweat forming on his brow.

"I'm not sure I care for your tone, Inspector. Are you *doubting* my abilities?"

"How can I doubt what I don't know you do?" she fired back at him without pause.

He sat forward in his chair and opened his diary. "Here's a usual day for me. This all happened on Friday of last week. Most of the morning was spent going over the various contracts I'm negotiating for some of my players who are without a club at the moment. Here's a prime example of what I do. One of my players wants to build an extension to his property. He needs a games room, of all things. Therefore it's my job to get quotes for him. Another player wanted a suit made for a wedding. Again, it's down to me to sort it out for him."

"I think I'm getting the picture now, and your fee would be?"

Russell smirked. "Generally it's ten per cent. From time to time, that figure will vary, depending on the player or club involved."

"So when a player needs an interior designer, of course you arrange for Ms. Styles to quote for a job, is that right?"

"That's right. Although I don't tend to put that kind of work out to tender. I know Danielle is the best around, so I tend to guide my players to use her services."

"In other words it's a win-win-win situation for you, what with you being a silent partner in the business and all."

"If you like," Russell said, grinning at her.

"So you're telling me, you do everything for these players apart from wipe their arses for them, is that right?"

His grin broadened, and he nodded. "I couldn't have put it better myself."

One more question, and then she'd hit him where it hurt. "What happens when one of your players gets caught drunk driving or something like that?"

He kept grinning. "It's muggins here who has to clear up the mess with your lot."

She gave him a killer smile. "That's what I thought. So you'll forgive me for wondering why you haven't felt the need to contact me over the past week."

"Sorry, I'm not with you," he said, looking confused.

"Let me refresh your memory. Last week, two of your players' houses were robbed. Dave Dobbs and Les Kelly, and yet, as SIO, I've never once been contacted by you with regard to the investigation. Why is that?"

Panic filled his eyes, and Lorne knew she had him by the short and curlies. He picked up his diary and swept back through the week, showing her how busy he'd been. "It's been a hell—of a fortnight," he stammered unconvincingly.

Then Lorne played her ace card. "I put it to you that you were behind these robberies and subsequent three murders. Therefore, Mr. Russell—or is it Trevor Murray?—I'm placing you under arrest."

Chapter Thirty-Two

AJ ran around the desk and slapped the handcuffs on Murray before he had the chance to reach for any likely weapon tucked away in his desk, while Lorne read him his rights.

"What the fuck? Are you out of your tiny little mind? Get yer fucking hands off me, pig."

Neither of the detectives responded to his foul-mouthed tirade as AJ marched Murray past his open-mouthed secretary and placed him in the back of the car.

Lorne drove. AJ sat in the back with the suspect just in case he tried to interfere with her while she was driving. She laughed when he kicked out in frustration at the back of her seat.

They reached the station. After instructing the desk sergeant to lock Murray in a cell and to notify his 'top' solicitor that he was in custody, Lorne headed up the stairs to fill Roberts in.

"That's great, and you're sure it's Murray?" Roberts asked, looking pleased by her accomplishment.

"I'm going to see if the pathologist can help us out there. Russell can swear till he's blue in the face that he's not Murray, but I'd bet a year's wages that I'm right."

"Can you get AJ or someone to check back to see if they have any photo ID of Murray before the supposed accident?"

"Good idea. If it's out there, we'll find it. He might even confess to it during questioning. Talking of which, how are you fixed? I thought you might like to sit in on the interview."

"You're not doubting yourself, are you?" he asked, quietly.

She grimaced. "I'm not doubting myself as such, but I'm conscious of the fact that I should've picked this guy up—or at least hauled him in for questioning—last week."

"These things are easily missed, and you've had a lot on your mind."

She closed her eyes and sighed. Those were the very words she didn't want to hear. The last thing she wanted was for him to think she wasn't up to the job. "Tony has nothing to do with this. Sean, as a friend, just help me ensure all the *T*s are crossed, *et cetera*, please?"

He gave an understanding nod. "Got you. It'll be like old times."

God, she hoped not; he used to be crap at interviewing. "Just to clarify, I'm still in charge of the interview. You'll be there to back me up, to prompt. *That's* all."

He had a glint in his eye and gave a nonchalant shrug. "But of course."

"We'll give his solicitor time to get here. In the meantime, I'll go prepare some questions."

"I have some paperwork to do anyway. Ring me when you're ready."

Stepping back into the incident room, she clapped to get the team's attention. "Listen up, guys. Drop what you're doing. We've got half an hour or so before I have to question Murray. I want everyone to concentrate on trying to find some kind of photo ID for Murray. I'm talking driving licence, passport, sports club membership—he looks as though he works out regularly—anything. I also want you to find out what his previous career was before he became an agent, and where Russell came from. My suspicion is that he appeared a couple of years ago after Murray's supposed disappearance. Tracy, any idea what's happening with regard to Ward?"

The young sergeant shook her head. "No, ma'am. He's totally disappeared."

"Okay, you can be sure if he knows or when he finds out the two Murray brothers have been picked up, he'll try and run. Molly, get onto the ports and issue an alert, *after* you see what you can find out about the IDs."

"Yes, ma'am."

"I'll be in my office."

Katy spoke as she passed her desk, "Do you want me to sit in on the interview with you?"

"No, that privilege is going to DCI Roberts, I'm afraid. I reckon he's going to be a slippery shit, so I asked the boss to sit in on it."

Katy smiled but didn't quite cover her disappointment. "I'll keep on top of the team, then."

Lorne thumped her lightly on the top of the arm. "Thatta girl."

Grabbing a coffee on the way, she settled down to sort out her interview questions. She'd just begun making notes when the phone rang. She picked it up. "DI Simpkins."

"It's Edwards."

She immediately dropped her pen and gave the caller her full attention. "Is it Tony? Is he all right?"

"Don't be alarmed. I just wanted to tell you that he's regained consciousness and is now off the critical list."

"Oh, thank God!"

"The medics in Basra are the dog's bollocks... Ahem... Sorry about that," he apologised after clearing his throat.

"No problem. I've heard far worse. When will he be fit enough to travel?"

"That's really why I'm ringing. He's coming home tomorrow. Four o'clock, he's due to touch down at Brize Norton. He asked me to let you know. Would you like to meet him?"

Lorne paused for a second or two to summarise how she saw the next couple of days panning out regarding the case. "I'm sure that'll be okay. It'll be wonderful to see him."

Awkwardly clearing his throat again, he said, "I'm sure it will. Take care."

She disconnected and instantly placed another call. "Patti, can you talk?"

"Lorne? Whatever is the matter? I've got two minutes before the next post."

"Keep it quiet, but Tony's coming home tomorrow. I'm so excited, I just had to tell someone."

Laughing, Patti's words matched her enthusiasm. "I'm so thrilled for you. We must arrange a celebratory drink, you know, when Tony feels up to it."

"That'd be excellent. Thanks again for your role in all this."

"Nonsense, I did nothing. I must go."

"Wait! We've arrested a suspect. I believe he's a guy who disappeared a few years ago and he's assumed another identity. Can you help at all?"

"If you can get the duty doctor to take a buccal swab for me, I can see if we can make a positive ID, providing we have a sample of his DNA in the system."

"Ah, now that's what I'm not sure about. He's part of a gang, but I think the other two members took the rap for any crimes they committed," Lorne said thoughtfully.

"That might cause a problem then. Send it over ASAP, and we'll see what we can do. Why don't you delve into his medical records?"

"Of course, just to see if his blood group is the same. He might be something other than a regular type O. You're a star, Patti. Speak soon."

She called out for Katy, who immediately appeared in the doorway. "Get the duty doc to get a buccal swab from Murray and a sample of blood, too. Then try and track down his medical records—both of them, Murray and Russell. We'll get the bastard one way or the other."

"Good idea. I'm on it." Smiling, Katy asked, "Everything all right? You look as though you've had some good news."

Winking, Lorne mouthed, "Tony's coming home tomorrow." Then she placed a finger to her lips.

Katy whispered, "That's brilliant news." She tapped her nose and left the room.

By the time Lorne had finished her list of questions and rang the DCI to join her, the team had found the one piece of incriminating evidence she needed to knock Murray off his confident pedestal.

Chapter Thirty-Three

Placing her notebook on the desk along with the brown envelope containing the pictures she'd shown his brother, Lorne sat in the seat opposite Murray-Russell.

DCI Roberts started the tape and named everyone in the room, including Russell's solicitor, Williams.

Lorne began, "Mr. Russell, for the tape, can you please tell us your connection with the footballers Dave Dobbs and Les Kelly?"

"They're my clients. I'm their agent."

"For how long?"

His mouth twisted before he answered. "A couple of years."

"Do you mind if we get to the point here. I have to be in court in a couple of hours, and if things progress any more slowly, I'm going to be late," Williams stated, offhandedly. All three of them gave him a dirty look, the harshest one coming from his own client.

"Fine by me. Mr. Russell—or would you rather me call you Trevor Murray? That is your real name, after all, isn't it?"

Williams looked up from his notebook, looking baffled. Lorne had to stifle a grin when he asked his client, "Is this true? Do you go by an alias?"

"Shut up," snapped Murray.

"Let me fill you in a little, Mr. Williams, on what we know about your charming client here." Lorne ran through what they'd uncovered about the suspect, and while she did so the amazed solicitor kept opening and shutting his mouth, like a fish out of water and gasping for air.

By the time she told the solicitor about the robberies and the murders, Murray was glaring at her in rage, giving her the impression that had they been alone, he would have quite happily throttled her.

"Sums it up nicely, doesn't it?" she asked the suspect.

He wrung his hands together in front of him. "You think you've got all this sussed, don't you, bitch?"

Sensing that DCI Roberts was about to stick up for her, Lorne touched him gently on the thigh. Then she took the photos of the crime scenes out of the envelope and slid them across the desk between the solicitor and his client. She watched Williams take a cursory glance at the photos and heard him gag. Murray smirked, making Lorne angry. *You callous bastard!*

Then she reached into the envelope again and brought out something the suspect hadn't been expecting. She thrust the picture from an old driving licence in the name of Trevor Murray before him. *Get out of that one, shitface.*

"It's hard to deny with proof as damning as that, isn't it?" Lorne said.

His brow furrowed for a time before he started smiling, a smile that sent shivers running up her spine. "So what?"

"What did you mean when you said 'You think you've got all this sussed'? Is there someone else connected to these crimes?"

She watched him chew the inside of his mouth as he debated whether to tell her or not. She didn't have to wait long.

Finally, he admitted, "The robberies weren't my idea."

"But you admit you and your gang were behind them?" Lorne asked, her heart thumping.

"My dumb brother has probably told you that already."

Lorne nodded. "So who was the brains behind this master plan of yours?"

"Before I tell you that, I want some kind of deal," Murray said.

Lorne nodded again.

Being smart, Murray said, "For the tape, Inspector."

She scowled at the suspect. It galled her to have to say it, but she knew if she didn't agree there was every chance the person would get away with it and possibly set up another gang to continue robbing and killing.

"You'll get a deal *if* the person you're about to name is apprehended."

"You've got to do better than that, Inspector."

Lorne glanced sideways at Roberts who gave a brief nod of encouragement. "Okay, you have my word that you'll get the best deal. Although with the severity of the crimes involved, I can't promise anything substantial. I'll do my best for you."

"Fair enough. You better get that little backside over to pick up Deb Brownlee, then."

"What? Are you serious?"

"Yep."

"Sir, can I see you outside for a moment?"

Roberts stopped the tape, and they both left the room. "I take it you know this Brownlee?" he asked once the interview room door was shut.

"I've never met her, but the day after the first robbery I rang her. Jesus, why didn't I go and see her in person?"

Ignoring her self-damnation, Roberts patted her on the shoulder. "I'll finish up here. You get over there and arrest her."

"If you're sure."

"*Go!*"

Chapter Thirty-Four

She didn't need telling a second time. Lorne bolted up the stairs to the incident room. "Katy, get ready to go."

Katy watched the whirlwind that was Lorne fly past her and into her office, returning a few seconds later with her coat on, ready to leave, and heading for the door.

"Where are we going?" Katy asked, running down the stairs after Lorne. She didn't receive the answer until they pulled out of the car park and into traffic.

"To the club. Murray just told me that Deb Brownlee is the one pulling his strings."

"Jesus!"

* * *

Thirty minutes later, they had conquered various traffic jams and reached Borthwick City's ground. Improvements were still being made at one end to comply with premiership rules, as the club had just gained promotion.

Moving swiftly through the glassed reception area, Lorne asked the young woman wearing gaudy eye makeup where the director's office would be located.

The woman instinctively reached for the phone. Lorne slammed her hand down on top of the woman's, preventing her from making the call. Showing her warrant card she said, "Just tell me where to go."

The woman's gaze shot several daggers in her direction before she finally pointed through the set of glass doors on the right.

"Thanks. I'd appreciate you *not* telling her we're on the way." She could say it, but she knew it was pointless. The minute they disappeared through the doors, the scary-eyed woman would be straight on the phone to warn Brownlee.

"Come on, Katy. Quick."

The glass doors led onto a long narrow hallway that had numerous glass offices on either side. At the very end, Lorne honed in on a large oak door, different from the others in the hallway, that had 'boss' door' written all over it. When they got nearer, the plaque indicated her suspicion to be correct. Without knocking, Lorne burst into the office. The woman sitting behind the large oval glass desk gave the impression she'd been expecting them.

"Can I help you?" Brownlee asked. Lorne suspected Brownlee's tone usually had men going weak at the knees. She swept her long mane of blonde hair over her shoulder and stood up. Coming from behind the desk, she held out a long bony, almost skeletal, red-varnished hand for Lorne to shake.

Ignoring it, she flashed her ID. "DI Simpkins and DS Foster. We'd like to ask you some questions."

The woman took a couple of steps back, perched her scrawny behind on the desk, and casually folded her arms. "About what?"

"About the recent robberies concerning a couple of your players."

"Ah, I remember. You rang me last week after David Dobbs' house was burgled. Unfortunate incident."

"It was indeed. Something that I've since learned you know more about than you led me to believe."

The woman's smile didn't falter. "I'm not sure I follow, Inspector."

"Maybe this will help you: At the moment, we have a couple of your associates either in prison or at the station giving interviews."

Still, the confident façade remained. "Associates? Associates in what, may I ask?"

"Have you heard from Stuart Russell lately, Ms. Brownlee?" Lorne asked, stepping closer to the woman, whose attitude was starting to tick her off.

She placed a slim finger to the side of her head, indicating that she was wracking her brain for a suitable date to appease them. "Um… Sometime last month, I believe. Why?"

"And the meeting was about?"

"What it's always about. A player, if I remember rightly."

Lorne shot back quickly, "That player wouldn't be Dave Dobbs, would it?"

Smiling broadly and blinking numerous times, something Lorne assumed Brownlee only did when she was nervous, she replied, "It might have been. I can't really remember."

Lorne gave the woman one of her 'Don't take me for an idiot' looks. "During the meeting, is that when you and Russell hatched the plan?"

An uncertain look crossed Brownlee's face, but the woman's laughing gaze riled Lorne. "Plan? What plan would that be?"

"The plan where you decided to rob the Dobbses and kill their children," she challenged. "And before you try denying it, Russell has already implicated you in the crime and told us everything."

"You're bluffing. He wouldn't dare."

"I think you'll find he has, and to save his own skin he volunteered your name as quick as that." She clicked her fingers together.

"You're trying to trick me."

"I'm not. He's being most cooperative. How else would we know you were involved?"

Momentarily, Brownlee looked flummoxed by her question. In the end, she held Lorne's gaze, and her mouth remained firmly shut.

"What I can't understand is why someone in your position would stoop so low?" Again, no response. So Lorne continued, "Was murder part of the plan?"

Brownlee's head dropped, and she continued to stare at the carpet a few feet in front of her.

"Do you have any kids, Ms. Brownlee? Have you got any idea what those poor people are going through right now? The guilt those two mothers will have to live with for the rest of their lives? Lorne's voice rose in anger with each question that went unanswered. "My God, woman, do you even *care*?"

The questions finally seemed to hit a nerve. Brownlee lifted her head, and her calm and collected persona vanished. She gave Lorne a venomous scowl. Baring slightly crooked teeth, she snarled, "Do I care? No, I don't fucking care. Why should I?"

Disgusted by the woman's ferocious outburst, Lorne shook her head. "Three innocent kids. Why?"

"I had no idea he was going to kill the kids, but—"

"No, don't tell me. When you heard about the murders, you thought they were a neat idea."

Brownlee shrugged.

"Why would you think such a thing? What harm have those women ever done to you?"

Instead of Brownlee answering Lorne's question, Katy did. "Envy. You were envious of them."

Lorne kept her gaze focused on Brownlee and watched her lip curl up again, her eyes sparkling with anger. "They don't deserve what they have."

"Who don't? The wives or the players employed by your club?" Lorne asked, confused.

"All of them. Some of these players are on more money a week than I earn in a year. All they do is kick a shitting ball around for ninety or one hundred and eighty minutes per week."

Disbelief made Lorne shake her head. "As opposed to you working your butt off for what, eighty hours a week?"

"That's right. Without *me*, this club wouldn't run like clockwork."

Lorne surveyed the office, which could only be described as minimalistic. The only items in the room were a corkboard on the wall behind Brownlee's chair that was full of postcards from exotic paradise isles, the desk, and her chair. Katy was right. The woman was bloody jealous.

"You're sick. You wanted those women to suffer long after the robbery. That's why you told Murray to kill the kids, wasn't it?" The smirk Brownlee gave her was enough to admit her guilt. Lorne took a step closer, menacingly, standing so close they were almost touching noses. "You'll get yours, Ms. Fancy Director. Your punishment won't only be your extensive prison sentence, but the women prisoners will take great pleasure in making sure you live with the guilt for the rest of your sorrowful life. One thing they can't stand is a child killer. Get the cuffs on, Sergeant, and read her rights to her."

* * *

That evening, after making sure both suspects were tucked up comfortably in their cells, the team set off to the White Horse for a quick celebratory drink.

Roberts popped in for a swift half to propose a toast, "To the best DI in town."

She blushed as the team cheered and called out her name before Roberts guided Lorne to a table by the window. "Not sure I agree with your announcement."

"Don't be so modest. You are the best DI the Met has, male or female."

"Then why didn't I arrest Russell and Brownlee sooner?"

"Lorne." Roberts warned. "Let me put it this way: If you hadn't made the connection with Underhill and Zac Murray, this case would *never* have been solved."

He had a point, but it didn't stop the guilt she was feeling. Or the relief that another family hadn't suffered in the way the Dobbses and Kellys had.

"Okay. I need to talk to you about where I go from here."

Roberts nodded but didn't appear too surprised by her statement. "Go on."

"I just wanted to prepare you, really. I'm still in the dark about what kind of care Tony is going to need when he returns. I think it would be best if I handed in my notice."

"Don't do anything rash. See how things are when he returns. You'll probably be grateful for the salary, if…"

She knew what he was reluctant to say. But Tony's needs would always come first from then on. Fair enough that if she had a 'normal' nine-to-five job, maybe she wouldn't think twice about jacking her job in; but being a copper wasn't just a career. It was a consuming way of life.

"We'll see. Anyway, at the rate DS Foster is tearing up the ranks, I can see her banging on your door in a few years, wanting to move up the pay scale."

They both looked over at Katy, who was sitting on a stool next to AJ, deep in conversation.

"So do you think she'll ever be as good as you?" Roberts asked with a furrowed brow.

"Honestly? I think she'll be even better. I'll always be around if she needs any advice in the future. We've both been through a lot together this past week. I have no reservations about the strength of her character and will to survive."

Roberts leaned into Lorne and whispered, "She reminds me so much of you, when you first joined. Of course, that'll have to stop before it gets going."

She smiled. "I'll have a word, although they do make a striking couple."

"Seriously, Lorne, whatever you decide to do, there will always be a job open on my team for you."

She punched his arm playfully. "Thanks, Sean. I appreciate that."

Chapter Thirty-Five

The following morning, Lorne stretched and cuddled Henry for a minute or two before the collie started whining to be let out. She'd had the best night's sleep she'd had in days, her mind restful now that she knew Tony was on his way home. She sang in the shower, something she rarely did, before she started tidying the house, making it all sparkly for his arrival.

Mid-morning she received two phone calls. The first was from Edwards, telling her that the plane had departed safely and was scheduled to land at four as arranged. The second was from her sister, Jade. "My God, Lorne, I'm so sorry. Dad rang me this morning to tell me about Tony."

"Did he? I didn't want you worrying. You have enough on your plate, sweetheart." Lorne threw herself down on the sofa, taking the opportunity to have a breather from the domestic chores.

"How will he cope? It's just awful. You're still getting married, aren't you?"

Lorne found herself shaking her head. When Jade got going, she could give the Gestapo a run for their money.

"I'll answer those in order. It remains to be seen, and yes, we're still getting married—at least, I hope so. Tony's injury might have caused him to have second thoughts on the matter." It was the first time she'd thought about that. Panic rose and constricted her chest. What if he couldn't bear her seeing him as an invalid? Who was to say what his reaction would be to his own injuries? What if he finished with her, told her to live life to the full with someone he considered better than himself? *What if... What if...*

"Don't do that. He'll be fine. You'll both help each other through this, to remain strong. He loves you so much, Lorne."

Sadly, Lorne reflected on the days she and Tony had spent walking on the beach in Brighton, with Henry barking as he waited for Tony to throw his ball into the sea. She sighed heavily. "I know he does. The mind is a powerful weapon, though. You hear such horror stories of how men react to…" She gave another sigh. "We'll see how it works out."

"Hey, as soon as Dad told me, I rang my mother-in-law. She's offered to take the kids off my hands for a few days so I can help out."

"Really? I'm not sure what you'll be able to do, hon. Like I said, I'm not certain if he'll be coming home or going on to a hospital when he lands. They haven't given me any details yet."

"I understand. Hey, I know—let me take over the wedding plans."

"I love your enthusiasm, but I don't want him to feel pressured into anything. We need to see how the land lies first."

"I disagree. I'll be over this morning to pick up your wedding folder. I'm in charge from now on, got it? You just concentrate on tending to your fiancé's needs."

Lorne knew better than to argue when Jade had her mind set on something. "Okay, you win. Look, I better get on. Speak soon, Sis."

They blew each other a kiss and hung up.

* * *

Lorne arrived at the gates to Brize Norton airfield at three thirty p.m. Good thing she got there early, as the plane touched down five minutes after.

With each bounce of the wheels hitting the tarmac, her heart leapt in her chest and dropped again until the wheels touched and the plane glided to a halt.

She was escorted to the C-130 Hercules. The large cargo door dropped open, and several men in combat uniforms disembarked, carrying the stretcher. Desperate to see Tony, she ran towards them, tears already welling up in her eyes behind the sunglasses she was wearing.

"Tony! My darling." She gasped when she saw the bruises covering his once handsome face. His head tilted when he heard her voice. He'd clearly been heavily sedated for the trip.

Somehow he managed to raise his hand off the stretcher. She grabbed it gently and let out a huge sigh. There were times when she had thought, rightly or wrongly, that day would never come.

He weakly tugged her arm bringing her closer so he could whisper in her ear. "I love you, princess." The medication made his words slur. "Don't leave me, will you?"

Her tears dripped onto his cheek. Removing her glasses, she pressed her lips onto his for the gentlest of kisses, afraid that she might hurt him. "Never. You're stuck with me forever, darling," she told him before exhaustion forced his eyes shut and he drifted off to sleep.

The officer in charge told her that usually, injured soldiers would be transferred to the hospital at Headley Court, near Dorking, but as Tony was MI6, he was being transported to the intensive care unit at The Manor Hospital, Oxford.

The next ten days Lorne spent sitting patiently at Tony's bedside. Sometimes his mood was good, and other times he spent hours silently reflecting. Occasionally, she caught him gazing down at his leg and wincing as though the event was running through his mind.

Finally, the doctors gave the all-clear to take him home. Henry, such a sensitive dog, didn't leave his side for the first twenty-four hours—well, only left his side for a wee.

Once home, Tony was near enough his old self again within a few days, even going so far as to make light of his injury. As he and Lorne cuddled up on the sofa together, he tilted her chin up and asked, "So are you still going to make an honest man out of me?"

"I was kind of avoiding the subject."

He looked shocked. "Why? Don't you want to marry me?"

She scrambled to sit upright and placed a hand on either side of his face. "Are you kidding? I'll ring Jade straight away."

"What's Jade got to do with it?"

"She took over the arrangements. She told me that no matter how sick you were that you'd still want to marry me."

"And she was right. So, when are we getting hitched?" he asked, giving her the widest smile ever.

"One minute." She rang Jade to ask how everything was proceeding, to be told that it was all in hand. All they had to do was turn up at the registrar's on Saturday at eleven a.m.

When she hung up, he looked at her expectantly with such love in his eyes that an involuntary shiver ran the length of her spine and tickled the back of her neck.

"Well?"

"Would you believe this Saturday?"

"Suits me. Come here." he pulled her, crushing her against him. Their kiss lingered long into the night.

Epilogue

Friends and family gathered at the registry office in Highbury that Saturday. Tony grimaced and battled with the pain to stand alongside her, adamantly refusing to get married in a wheelchair. Jade had done a wonderful job and hadn't forgotten a single aspect to their special day. Charlie looked amazing in her two-piece blue trouser suit, and Lorne looked beautiful in her ivory skirt suit that finished just above the knee, showing off her shapely legs.

She had helped Tony get into his new navy blue suit that morning, and was so proud of the way he held himself up on the crutches during the ceremony.

The reception took place at The Gifford Hotel in the small banqueting suite for select small gatherings such as theirs. While Lorne was circulating, mixing with the guests, someone lightly tapped her on the shoulder. "Patti! I'm so glad you could make it. Grab a drink from the waiter, and I'll introduce you to Tony. Is Dave with you?"

Patti looked to the left, and Lorne's gaze followed hers to where Tony sat in his wheelchair, laughing and shaking a stocky man's hand. "He's reacquainting himself with Tony now, I think."

"No! Was it Dave who rescued him?"

The two women joined their partners and made the necessary introductions. Dave held out his hand for Lorne to shake, but she instead pulled him into her arms and kissed his cheek. "Thank you for bringing Tony home safely."

Stepping back, he mock saluted. "It's all part of the service, ma'am."

She shook her head. "You went above and beyond, and I'll be forever in your debt."

Because Tony's wounds still needed constant medical care, the honeymoon was delayed until he was fully recovered. So they spent the following week mostly in bed.

"What's happening about work? Have you decided yet?" Tony asked over scrambled eggs and toast one morning.

"Actually, I have. We're going to sell this house and the flats that we renovated and buy a house in the country."

"Oh, we are, are we?"

"Yes. We're also going to buy ten acres of land, or thereabouts, and we're going to set up an animal sanctuary of some kind."

Laughing, he wiped his mouth with the napkin. "You have it all worked out in that pretty little head of yours, don't you?"

"I do, indeed." And if the Met came calling for her services again in the future, she'd tell them she was otherwise engaged.

Printed in Great Britain
by Amazon.co.uk, Ltd.,
Marston Gate.